A RIPPLE IN TIME

David Berardelli

A RIPPLE IN TIME

GRAVESTONE PRESS

CHAPTER ONE

Like most large cities, Pittsburgh celebrates the Christmas season on a grand scale.

Tinsel and garlands decorate lamp posts and traffic lights. Bright blinking lights and glittering decorations embellish storefront windows. Wreaths and giant candy canes garnish the entrance doors of restaurants and many other businesses, and artificial snow gathered tastefully at the bottom of window displays blends in with snowflakes sprinkling various portions of the glass.

It was seasonably cold when I got out of my rented gray Challenger on Liberty Avenue and went down the block that brought me to Gino's Bar & Grill at eight o'clock that night. Liberty Avenue had been one of my favorite haunts when I lived here more than twenty years ago, before graduating from Carnegie-Mellon and earning my degree in Business Administration. I'd spent much of my spare time in this area during those four years and couldn't wait to see how much it had changed.

I hadn't been back to the Tri-state area since the day I'd left. After being offered a key position with the new Orlando consulting firm, Crosley, Williams, and Associates, as their new Administrative Director, I'd moved to Winter Park, Florida, and had lived there ever since.

It had been a smart move on my part. I became their Executive Director in eight years, earning my place as junior partner with the firm just three years later. The company was now called Crosley, Williams, Danner, and Associates, and along with a terrific salary, an impressive stock portfolio and a benefits package to die for, I'd achieved in just a decade and a half what most people dream about all their lives.

Since I hadn't been back in two decades, I'd never been in Gino's before. I was staying at the Fairmont Hotel on Market Street. They had a terrific bar called Andy's, but after my plane trip, I wanted to stretch my legs and satisfy my curiosity by checking out the "new" Liberty Avenue.

I vaguely remembered that the building that was now Gino's had once been a sandwich shop, takeout pizza, and a Chinese restaurant during the four years I was enrolled at Carnegie-Mellon. It was also a travel agency for a few months.

Gino's was bustling when I entered the place. Like the rest of the block, it was decorated richly for the holidays. A six-foot pine tree glorified the foyer just a few feet from the front entrance and in full view of the front window. The tree was decorated with Hallmark originals as well as antique toys and trimmings I hadn't seen since I was a kid growing up in Gibsonia, a small rural town just twelve miles north of the city. Garlands hung loosely across the beamed ceiling, starting at the entrance and extending the entire length of the long, narrow room. Mistletoe dangled in strategic spots.

Since many of the patrons already appeared drunk and happy, I kept clear of the mistletoe while inching my way to the long, U-shaped bar. I wasn't in the mood to be groped and kissed sloppily by drunken women I didn't even know. I didn't feel safe until I'd squeezed my butt onto a stool between a big guy in a suit and a middle-aged woman discussing crooked politics with her date, a slender man around sixty or so wearing a cheap green suit and an ill-fitting blond toupee.

The barman, a big-boned Italian with piercing black eyes, thinning black hair and a thick black mustache, shuffled right over. I ordered a vodka and tonic and smiled when the crowd noise hushed for a few moments when Bing Crosby began singing "White Christmas" from the corner juke.

The barman brought over my drink long before I expected it and placed it carefully onto a brown coaster with *GINO'S* monogrammed in fancy black script in its center. I slid a five in his direction, picked up the glass and sipped. It was strong, and warmed me instantly. I could clearly feel the jet lag subsiding and sighed as my limbs relaxed and the rest of me warmed up and melted comfortably into the soft leather cushion of the seat.

The barman brought me back change and dropped it on the counter next to my glass. "You no live here?" he asked in a strong, low-pitched voice I could hear clearly over Bing's distant mellow crooning.

"How could you tell?"

He grinned, showing a mouthful of large yellow teeth. "Ya look like ya just got in from somewhere else. 'Sides, I don't see many hundred-dollar ties come in here." He nodded, pleased with himself. "Yep, definitely outa town."

I smiled. The man certainly was observant.

He tilted his head. "Am I right?"

"Dead-on."

7

He chuckled. "So...this your first time in town?"

"I lived here a long time ago."

"Where?"

"I grew up in Gibsonia."

"How long ago ja leave?"

"Last time I was here, this place was Chinese takeout."

He shrugged. "We been here ten, twelve years, now. This was *way* before, yes?"

"A few years."

"Move away?"

I nodded. "Florida, about twenty years ago."

"No like the winters here?"

"I didn't mind the winters too much. I was offered a good job in Orlando. I've been there ever since."

"Miss it here?"

"Once in a while."

"Family still here?"

"My parents split up a long time ago. Last I heard, my father's in North Carolina. My mom's remarried and living somewhere in Arizona. I flew up here for a business meeting with some people who run a company on Smithfield."

He was squinting, trying to absorb all this. "So...ya came all the way from Florida for a *business meeting*? On *Christmas*?"

"It was kind of a spur-of-the-moment decision. On their part—not mine."

The barman squinted, obviously confused. "I thought everything was done on the phone these

8

days." He shrugged. "Email? Online? All that other technology crapola?"

I laughed. "You're right about that."

"What's different with this?"

"When it's a big deal like this one, some people like the old-fashioned one-on-one. And, of course, the handshake once the deal's been made. With drinks later on, of course."

He nodded.

I didn't want to tell him that even though I had no prior intention of returning to Pittsburgh, I really didn't mind spending Christmas here. Since I'd recently broken up my eight-month romance with Sarah, I had no one to spend Christmas with. So, when my boss Sam Crosley asked me to make the trip as a personal favor to him, I agreed without hesitation. Upon reflection, I guessed that the breakup bothered me more than I'd originally thought, urging me to keep my mind occupied with work during the holidays.

"How's it feel to be home again?" the barman asked.

Even during my brief trip from the Fairmont to Liberty Avenue, I noticed how much this place had changed in twenty years. Many of the old buildings had been torn down and replaced with new ones. At least the Gulf Building looked the same. I suspected it always would. Even so, I experienced an unexpected sadness for leaving home, moving nearly a thousand miles away and never once looking back. It might have been different if my parents hadn't split up and left home…

9

But they had. And in doing so, they'd robbed me of many of my fondest memories.

"I don't know yet." I didn't want to insult him by telling him I'd stopped considering Pittsburgh my home a long time ago. "I just got off the plane."

"Well, I hope your stay's a good one." Then he went off to tend to another customer.

I took another sip of my drink and scanned the room. People were getting sloppier, staggering around on the dance floor in the back and making out at their tables. One woman had half the buttons of her frilly white blouse undone and didn't seem to notice. Her date, on the other hand, couldn't take his eyes off the exposed bra. The juke was now playing Andy Williams' version of "*Christmas Present*."

Briefly I wondered if I should have another drink or just drive back to the Fairmont, have one last drink at Andy's, and relax in my room until morning. I'd never been a heavy drinker, although I'd gone through occasional spells during the last few years when I'd hit the bottle more often than I should have. Life often dealt unexpected blows. When it did, you reacted by doing stupid things, like buying a sports car, growing a beard, or jumping the bones of a woman young enough to be your daughter.

In my case, I just drank more than usual.

Nonetheless, I considered myself a solid, stand-up sort of guy. Although I was a charter member of the social circle at Crosley, Williams, Danner, and Associates, I rarely went out drinking with them. I went to whatever function was scheduled and did what I was required to do. But instead of spending

10

the night with half a dozen or so rowdy drinkers, I invariably drove back to my Winter Park condo and spent the rest of the evening alone, watching an old movie with a small glass of vodka tonic or port wine.

The barman came back and glanced at my glass. When he saw that it was half-empty, he said, "Ya come here alone?"

"I always travel alone."

"No wife? No kids?"

"No."

He looked surprised. "A prosperous, good-lookin' guy like you?"

I shrugged. "I'm not that easy to live with."

He boomed laughter. "Hear ya, buddy! Hear ya!" Then, still chuckling, he went over to tend to someone else at the other end of the bar.

I'd been engaged three times and had dated at least twenty different women in the last twenty years. I had no idea why none of these relationships had turned out. I always seemed to be searching for a particular type of woman I knew did not actually exist, a woman I saw only in my dreams. I'd had my share of teenage crushes, but when I developed into an adult living in the real world, all my early fantasies seemed to vanish into the dust. I was a big boy in a world filled with real people, and that meant something totally different from what I'd dreamed about all those years as a young man expecting a lifelong romance with some faceless woman living only in my imagination.

A few minutes later, just as Mel Torme broke into his "*Christmas Song*" from the juke, I finished

11

my drink and decided to shift back into the real world of the here and now. I had to drive back to the Fairmont and wanted to do it sober. I'd only actually driven drunk a couple of times before and knew how difficult and unpleasant it was to handle a moving vehicle in heavy traffic. My memory of Pittsburgh cops was one of caution and sincere respect. I was in no mood to be pulled over and take my chances submitting to a breathalyzer.

I left a tip, waved to the barman as I got down from my stool, and left the loud, Christmas-filled room.

I went back out into the cold night. Pulling up the collar of my overcoat to shield my ears and the back of my neck from the freezing night air, I went back to the Challenger. Not too many people were out. I figured they were probably in the bars or at the restaurants.

I got out my keys and pressed the remote to unlock the door. A moment later, something hard was shoved into my lower back just as I took one last step toward the driver's door.

"The keys, asshole!"

The voice was high-pitched, raspy, and much too close for comfort. I caught a strong whiff of weed and the faint scent of whiskey.

I held out the keys. They were immediately snatched from my grasp, jarring my left shoulder. I was about to protest when whatever was pressing against me jabbed me harder, sending a jolt of hot pain up my spine. "*And* the wallet. *Now*!"

I made a move for my wallet and was immediately jabbed even harder. I gasped when another spike of hot pain raced up my spine.

"Dammit!" Despite the frightening situation, the anger spewed out from me. I was trying to cooperate, to comply with my assailant's demands. There was no need for the bastard to be so rough. "I'm trying to get it, so hold your water—"

"Shuddup!" He slammed me against the side of the rental and moved even closer to me. His face was inches from the back of my neck. I could tell he was much shorter than I was. But it wasn't his height that concerned me. It was whatever he was ramming into my lower back. "I don't want any shit from you, asshole—just your goddamn wallet!"

I wanted to turn around and deck him but didn't know if he was holding a gun, knife, or blackjack. I also didn't know in which hand he held the weapon. I remembered that this one factor was crucial in a defense-type situation. I'd studied unarmed combat in college but never had the opportunity to practice or apply it. Since I'd turned forty-two earlier this year and began suffering from sciatica, I was in no shape for any sudden foolish Bruce Lee-type heroics. I decided to just give him what he wanted and hoped he'd slither back to his rock the instant he got what he wanted.

I tried once again to reach into my pocket for my wallet. As I did, whatever he kept poking me with pressed firmly into the small of my back again. "Faster!" he whispered fiercely, and another miasmatic blend of weed and whiskey assaulted my nostrils.

I gritted my teeth as I grabbed the wallet, pulled it out and held it out.

Without a word he snatched it from my grasp.

I stood perfectly still, anxiously waiting—hoping—to hear him running away.

Instead, I heard approaching footsteps.

My heart practically jumped out of my chest. Could this possibly be a cop coming to my rescue? Was it someone from the street witnessing my predicament and rushing over to help?

Was I about to be saved after all?

Just as I expected to hear something like, "Police! Freeze!" I heard someone whisper, "We need to get the fuck outa here, Jake!"

Before I could react, something hard whacked me on the back of my skull.

Blackness consumed me.

14

CHAPTER TWO

When I came to, the back of my head pounded, and my joints felt as if they'd been crushed.

I lay on my back on the cold hard ground, my arms and legs totally numb. Before I opened my eyes, I took a breath and nearly choked on the rancidness hovering about in the air. The heavy mix of rotting food, urine, and machine oil was nauseating. I was obviously lying near a dump, or in an alley behind a restaurant, where discarded food was tossed in a dumpster and left there until it was picked up by the city.

A flurry of high-pitched voices penetrated the cold night air not far from where I lay. They sounded like older kids, perhaps in their late teens. They were laughing and carrying on. It made me wonder if they were having some sort of party. I wanted to open my eyes and explore my surroundings, but some inner voice told me to lie perfectly still, and keep my eyes shut.

Then, during my confusion, I heard footsteps. They grew louder as they crunched gravel in my direction. When they were just a few feet away, they stopped. The high-pitched voice of a young teen standing a foot or so on my right reverberated in my ears. "I want his suit!"

"What the hell for?" came another voice about twenty or thirty feet away, also on my right. It sounded like the bastard who'd held me at gunpoint on Liberty Avenue. I vaguely recalled someone calling him Jake. "Goin' to a party?"

"I want it! The coat, too!"

"Sucker's *way* too big for ya, Jonesie!" yelled another kid. "Ol' fart's a foot taller than you! You'd have to cut it up to fit!"

"I'll grow into it!"

Snickers.

"Just wait," said Jake.

"Fer what?" asked Jonesie, who was now standing near my feet. "He won't need it no more!"

"We'll dump 'im first," replied Jake. "*Then* you can have the damn suit!"

"The coat, too?"

"Yeah, whatever…"

"What about his shoes?"

"Take the shoes, dammit. I don't give a shit."

A chuckle. The kid standing on my right side said, "Sucker's loaded. Those shoes go for a coupla hundred!"

Jonesie said, "There's twelve hundred and five cards in his wallet!"

Then I heard a fourth voice. This one seemed to be coming from where Jake was. "We max out the cards, mebbe get another five K."

"Not bad for one night," Jake said.

"Don't forget the wheels," the kid on my right said. "Mebbe five hundred, once we get 'er stripped."

Jake said, "We gotta take 'er to 'Sliberty, we want that much. Bugger likes choppin' muscle cars."

Jonesie bent over me. "I get your suit, asshole," he whispered, sending a heavy cloud of weed into my nostrils. "The coat, too." Then he shifted on the pavement and walked away.

I realized right then that I had to do something. I couldn't just lie here and let them do whatever they wanted. My head pounded, my arms and legs were numb with pain and cold, and my spine had become one large mass of hot, jagged pain. But I refused to just lie here and let a pack of young hoodlums kill me, steal my money and clothes, and take my rented Challenger to have it stripped bare.

But what on earth could I possibly do?

Baby steps, I told myself. They'd just left me alone. I needed to survey my surroundings.

Since I was lying in the dark, they couldn't see me very well. Cautiously I opened my eyes and slowly turned my head a few inches in their direction.

Four dark figures sat cross-legged in a semicircle about forty feet away, eating food from paper bags. Facing them, jagged golden flames flickered brightly from the mouth of a gutted trashcan. About twenty feet behind them, a dumpster overflowing with garbage sat near the brick wall of an ancient four-story building. A line of brick buildings extended as far as I could see. At the far end, brief glints of headlights lit up the mouth of the alley as traffic whizzed by.

As I scanned my surroundings, I struggled to get circulation back in my arms and legs as subtly as possible. Although I was reasonably sure I couldn't be seen, I remained still. Right now, the thugs were preoccupied with their meal. Even so, a couple of them glanced in my direction every so often.

I began opening and closing my hands into tight fists, all the while tightening my thigh muscles and wiggling my toes inside my shoes. Everything hurt at first, but I forced myself to keep up the procedure. After a few minutes, I began to feel as if I'd actually restored some of the feeling in my limbs. I didn't know how much time I had left but figured I was safe while they were eating. I had to do as much as I could as quickly as possible.

As I kept up my exercises, I turned my head slightly to the left. It took me only a moment to realize that my options were limited. I lay just a few feet from the back seat of a van, or pickup. I couldn't see anything behind it but was reasonably sure that the mouth of the alley leading back to the street extended beyond it. To escape, I'd have to jump up and maneuver around the seat. Then, gambling on the chance that nothing behind it would cause me to stumble or trip, I'd have to keep up a pace fast enough to outrun four teenage kids.

I was forty-two years old. The image of a guy my age outrunning four teens, under other circumstances, would be laughable.

I was doomed, plain and simple. I couldn't even see what lay on the other side of the seat or in front of it. The darkness hid from view anything that might serve as a suitable weapon.

But even though I knew I was facing the impossible, I still had to do something.

While considering my other limited options, I continued making fists, tensing my thighs, and wiggling my toes. After a short while, I began turning my hands at the wrists as well as turning my feet at the ankles.

As I slowly brought back my circulation, I decided that I should try and move closer to the salvaged bench seat. I knew I was in no shape to overpower four young punks living off the streets, but I could try and make this much more difficult for them by grabbing the seat and tossing it at them when they came at me. They were most definitely all armed, but they hadn't given me much of a choice. If I could hurt at least one of them before they murdered me, I'd have the satisfaction of taking that small but significant triumph to my grave.

A few minutes later, when I felt reasonably fit enough to attempt to slide closer to the seat, one of them belched loudly and tossed a paper bag into the fire.

My pulse thundered. I was running out of time. I had to do something now, before the others finished their meal.

Once again, I turned my head slightly to the left and began calculating distances. I figured six, maybe seven feet from my body to where the seat sat on the ground. The seat itself was nearly parallel to my position. If I could move closer to it, use it to prop myself up and then circle around it, I might be able to get a good enough hold on the bottom to yank it up and let it slam into them. It was probably much heavier than it looked, but I knew all about adrenaline and how it worked in a stressful situation. Besides, it was my only alternative.

19

Six, maybe seven feet to the seat... That would take approximately five seconds. Then another five to prop myself up, five more to circle the seat, bend over, take a grip on the bottom, grit my teeth, then let it fly—

Something else thumped into the flaming can, startling me again. Cautiously I turned my head. A second thug had tossed his bag into the fire and began lighting a cigarette. "Hurry up, you two," he said. "Haven't got all night!"

It was now or never.

Just as I prepared myself mentally to roll over toward the seat, the other two tossed their bags into the fire and got to their feet. All four were facing me now. Even though I was hidden in darkness, they'd see me moving away. But I had no other choice.

I took a deep breath. Then, tensing my arms and legs, I prepared myself to begin my hasty retreat.

But just then, I heard a soft voice very close to my ear. It was the voice of a young woman. "Don't move."

I froze.

Was there a *fifth* thug?

Was this gang run by a female? Was she also armed?

I knew better than crane my head around to see for sure, but something told me to remain still. Some inner sense—that same feeling that told me to keep my eyes closed—told me to do exactly as she said. A strange soothing quality in her voice told me she wasn't one of them. I strongly suspected that she wanted to help me.

The foursome started coming my way.

***

My pulse pounded deafeningly.

Visions of my death filled my head with darkness. Cold tingles crawled up my spine.

I couldn't just lie here and let them do me in. Voice or no voice, I had to fight—or find a weapon—or lash out with my fists. I had to do *some*thing.

I just couldn't die this way!

The four of them kept coming.

If I could just find something to hit them with...

I hadn't seen anything lying on the ground near me, but that didn't mean I should give up. Since there were no lamp posts to light up the area, the ground surrounding me remained totally black. For all I knew, there could be *something* lying around. This was an *alley*, for God's sake. Anything could be lying on the ground just a few feet away. A chunk of rock or brick might be lying just inches from my head. If I could just reach around me and pick it up... I could use it to bash one of them in the face...

If I could just find *some*thing...

Just then, their footsteps stopped at the same time.

My heart skipped a beat.

For long, agonizing moments, the four punks stood stock-still.

"'Ja hear that?" one of them whispered.

"Yeah. What the hell *was* it?"

"Damn if *I* know…"

"Prob'ly a rat."

"*Hate* fuckin' rats!"

"Don't think it was no rat…"

"What else could it—"

The sound of something thumping onto metal a few yards behind them made them all go silent.

For ten seconds, I could hear a pin drop. Then:

"What the *fuck*?"

"Somethin' over there, near the dumpster."

"Jonesie, go check it out."

"Hey, dude…I ain't goin' over there by myself!"

"Pussy... Chopstick, you'n that pussy check it out."

"What if—"

"Just *go*, dammit!"

"What about—"

The sound of something else thumping, this time onto a hollow surface, reverberated farther down the alley.

Once again, they all froze.

"Damn!"

"Shit!"

The click of a gun hammer echoed loudly.

"Some stupid shit's movin' around over there, and he's gonna get 'is ass popped!"

"Comin' with ya."

"Me, too!"

"I'm comin', too!"

"What about *this* bastard?"

"You stay here, Naddy. We won't be long."

22

"What if he comes to? Want me to finish 'im off?"

One of them pulled something out of his belt. "Hit 'im in the head with this. It'll keep 'im quiet till we get back."

A short crowbar changed hands. My heart sputtered. Then the other three moved out of my range of sight.

The kid with the crowbar stood over me, watching me.

I knew better than move a muscle.

My fear suddenly mixed with anger. I tensed up again. I couldn't just lie here and wait for this punk to make the first move. The moment he turned away to watch his friends, I began making fists again, gathering even more circulation and strength. *Mind over matter*... I remembered some psychology courses I'd taken in college when I was trying to learn about myself and my mental capabilities.

When the mind is in control, nothing is impossible.

If you concentrate properly, you cannot fail.

The punk was now looking down at me. I closed my eyes almost all the way, keeping them open a fraction so I could watch his movements in the darkness. He was holding the crowbar in his left hand and rubbing its curved head with his right—as if speculating what he should do with it.

He knelt and placed it on the ground on his left. Before I could figure out what he was about to do, he reached for the knot of my tie. Then, chuckling, he began loosening it.

The crowbar was just a foot from my head. It lay on his left, almost behind his body. To get to it, I'd have to turn on my right side, reach up and push him down. Since he was kneeling over me, the leverage factor requiring me to perform this simple task was quite possibly much more than I could handle right now. I was forced to lie there and let him strip me of the eighty-dollar, hand-sewn cotton tie Sarah had given me for my last birthday.

About half a minute later, he stopped loosening my tie and froze. Gasping, he spun around. "What the—" He groped for the crowbar, picked it up and jumped to his feet. "Who the fuck's there?"

I opened my eyes. He was standing a couple of feet on my right, scanning the alley on my left. He held the crowbar almost straight out in front of him.

"All right, shithead," he whispered. "Wanna be funny? C'mon out!"

A moment later, something dropped onto the ground several yards to my left, startling us both. I managed not to move, but he jumped nearly a foot in the air. Without a word, he stepped around me and quietly crept toward the mouth of the alley.

I turned just as the skinny figure disappeared into the darkness. Then I shook myself to see if I was able to move around.

Just then, I heard the young woman's voice again. As before, it sounded just a few inches away. "Can you get up?"

I nodded.

"Do it. You don't have much time."

I rolled onto my left side. Then, gritting my teeth, I struggled to kneel. A moment later, I was able to straighten. I wanted to turn around and see who was talking to me but suspected no one was there. But that didn't matter. It didn't even seem to matter that I could be hallucinating. I knew a little about head wounds and realized that such a thing often caused the victim to hear strange voices. But I could think about that later. Right now, I had to get away, and if it took a disembodied voice to help me do it, then so be it.

Once I'd straightened, wooziness took over. The ground at my feet shifted, and I felt faint. Taking a breath, I grabbed onto the back of the seat and braced myself, swaying a little until my equilibrium returned. Then I turned to my left.

The voice whispered, "You can't go out that way. You'll need to get to that dumpster. There's a door going into the building directly behind it. It's open, but you'll have to be careful. It's littered with junk and quite a few bums sleeping in the hall. Can you make it?"

I nodded.

"C'mon, then. I'll be with you all the way."

"Who *are* you?"

"Move, and don't stop until I tell you to."

I didn't have to be told twice. In seconds I'd crossed the alley on legs that refused to bend because they were numb with cold.

CHAPTER THREE

The hall in the rundown building was as black as the inside of a tomb.

It was a confined space and smelled much worse than the alley. The air, heavy with a disgusting reek of urine, feces, alcohol, vomit and rotting food, assaulted my nostrils and made my eyes water. I wiped them and forced myself to breathe through my mouth.

The total darkness made it impossible to distinguish anything straight ahead. I stood frozen in the open doorway, my heart pounding, my limbs shaking from fear and from the cold. The uncertainty of my fate—and the mortal danger lurking behind me—made me tremble. I hadn't heard the woman's voice since I'd come inside. I began to wonder if I'd just imagined it.

But just as I experienced another wave of cold fear welling up within me, I heard their voices in the alley not far from where I was standing. I risked a glance behind me and cringed. Four hazy shadows had gathered about sixty feet farther down, where they'd dumped me. They were arguing with one another, trying to keep their voices low. I had no idea what they were saying but guessed they were wondering where I'd gone. They'd no doubt soon begin their search.

My growing fear turned my blood cold. Despite my will to survive, I realized to my horror that my mind had gone blank. Complete darkness awaited me straight ahead. Entering it would be just as terrifying as turning around, stepping back outside, and facing the four punks.

Just then, I heard her voice again.

Once again, it sounded very close.

"Take three steps and turn just a little to your right. There's someone lying in the hall. You've got a couple of feet of space between his shoes and the wall where you can pass. Use the wall to guide you."

I did exactly as she said.

The moment I'd cleared the sleeping figure, she spoke again. "Walk eight steps and turn right. There's a broom closet. The door's closed. It opens from the right. Find the doorknob, pull it open, slip inside and close it quietly behind you. You can hide there until I tell you it's safe for you to leave."

"But how do you—"

"Do it *now*."

The urgency in her voice alarmed me, so I did as she said. After a few awkward moments of sliding my hand along the uneven surface of the weathered door, I found the cold doorknob, turned it and opened the closet door just a couple of seconds before I heard approaching footsteps not far behind me.

The closet was tiny and smelled extremely foul. Once again I forced myself to breathe through my mouth. The moment I gently eased the door closed, I turned, groped blindly at the space and, experimenting carefully, discovered a pile of boxes and what felt like garbage bags filling the tiny room.

"Squeeze behind them," the voice said next to me. "Then drop to your knees. There's enough clutter in here to hide you."

Without protest, I did exactly as she said.

Five seconds later, the door opened.

A tiny flashlight beam lit up the cramped space.

***

I froze.

Agonizing silence consumed the minuscule space. The flashlight beam darted in every conceivable direction, moving in a hectic, jerky fashion. As I squatted quite close to the boxes stacked in front of and around me, I willed myself to become part of the pile so I wouldn't be noticed.

Just when I thought I was about to come out of my skin, the beam lowered to the floor on the right side of the stack and remained still.

"Smells like shit in here," one of them whispered, sniffing.

"Bums took over," a second voice whispered. "Whaddya expect?"

"Didn't think that ol' fart would be in here."

"Was worth a look," the other one said.

"Waste a time. He'd never be able to move around."

"Sucker's pissin' his pants. He'd try anything to get away."

"'Ja find a flashlight when ya went through his pockets?"

A pause. "Nope…"

"See how dark it is in here?" The flashlight beam switched off. "He'd have to have X-ray-fuckin'-vision to get around…" The beam switched back on.

"Guess you're right…"

"Ya *think*?"

"But he's gotta be *some*wheres…"

"That's what we're gonna do right now, moron. Sucker couldn'ta got far. We'll find 'im."

The beam disappeared. The door slammed shut.

The footsteps out in the hall gradually diminished.

I waited tensely for the voice of the young woman to come back.

As I waited, the heavy silence ripped into me.

After nearly five minutes, I felt the panic returning. Here I was, squatting in the miniscule storage closet of an old building in the dead of night with a pack of vicious street thugs hunting me down. Judging from what they'd already done, I knew they'd kill me the moment they found me, and there wasn't much I could do to prevent them from doing it.

Since I had no light, I couldn't very well sort through the boxes in front of me for a weapon. Judging by the smell, I wouldn't want to. I couldn't waste precious time feeling for a light switch. Even if power somehow existed in the building, flicking on a light would send them here in moments.

I had no choice but remain in darkness. My back was killing me, my joints were screaming in agony, my feet were frozen, and the throbbing in the back of my head was getting progressively worse. It would be only a matter of time before I'd pass out.

My only salvation was the strange, disembodied voice that had managed to get me away from them. But right now, I wasn't even sure if I'd actually heard a voice or if it was just my imagination. I'd been hit over the head; I'd undoubtedly suffered a concussion. My imagination could have kicked in, fabricating much of this nightmare. For all I knew, the voice I kept hearing existed only in my head, and since I hadn't heard it in several minutes, I wasn't sure if I'd ever hear it again.

Struggling once again to keep the panic at arm's length, I took a deep breath and told myself to relax and try to somehow hold it all together. All I had to do was wait another few minutes. If I didn't hear anything, I might be able to get out of here. I was a business executive; I'd faced traumatic situations before. I knew my best bet was to treat this as an extreme emergency, but if I kept the panic at bay and maintained a clear head, I'd undoubtedly prevail.

My first step, of course, was to feel my way out of the closet and down the hall. Although I couldn't actually see anything, that didn't make the process impossible. I was at a definite disadvantage but was quite sure my adrenaline would help me—

"I'm glad you're still here," she said, her voice close.

I wanted to rejoice when I heard her. It took me two tries to find my own voice. "I thought…I was afraid I'd just …imagined you."

"Don't worry. You didn't."

"I'm really glad. Where were you?"

"I was making sure they weren't coming back here."

"Are they?"

"No. But that doesn't mean they won't later on."

"I was just about to try and get out of here."

"You can't go anywhere without a flashlight, you know."

"I didn't know what else to do. I didn't know if you'd come back—"

"I understand. But I do have to leave again. Wait here."

My heart fluttered. I *hadn't* imagined the voice after all.

"Thank you," I whispered.

Silence. My heart sank. She'd already gone.

I spent the next couple of minutes trying to figure out who she was and what was going on.

I also wondered if I was dead.

Or had gone stark-raving mad.

***

At least five more bone-chilling minutes later, I heard her again.

This time, her voice sounded like it was just a few feet straight ahead, on the other side of the pile of boxes and trash I was hiding behind.

"They left the building, but they're still close. Right now, they're checking another section of the alley. Come out of there and I'll guide you."

"I hope you realize I can't see a damned thing."

"It doesn't matter. I can see everything."

Her simple statement made me wonder once again just who she was and why I couldn't see her.

It also made me wonder why she was helping me. Logic told me that if she was actually trying to help, she must know me. Or maybe she just didn't like street punks.

In any event, if she knew me, she would have already told me who she was.

"Who *are* you?" I couldn't help asking. The suspense was driving me crazy.

"No time for that. You really need to get out of here right now."

"But like I said—"

"Take two side steps to your left and one small step straight ahead. Then make a right at about a forty-five-degree angle. It should only take you another step or two to get back out into the hall."

I did as she instructed, moving slowly and carefully, my right hand held straight out, groping for obstacles. My right shoulder bumped against the wall, jarring me. I felt for the doorway and used both hands to examine the inner edge of the door. Then I took two more steps and inched my way through the doorway.

Just as I stepped back out into the hall, she said, "Turn right, take five steps, then stop."

"Then what?"

"I'll tell you when you get there."

Once again I did as she instructed. Then I stopped after the required five steps.

"A body's lying right there in front of you," she said.

Had I heard her correctly? Did she say *body*? As in *corpse*?

"A *body*? Or a bum sleeping it off?"

32

"He's a bum, all right, but he's dead. By the smell, I'd say he's been dead a few days."

I took a whiff and immediately felt nauseous. "I don't know if I can—"

"He's skinny," she said.

Once again, I wondered if I'd heard her correctly. "What does that have to do with—"

"It makes him narrow. All you need to do is raise your right leg about a foot. Then bring it back down a foot and a half straight ahead. That should give you enough space to clear him. Once you do that, do the same thing with your other leg. You'll be good to go."

"I don't know if I can—"

"Do it."

The authority in her voice unnerved me. Despite my reservations, I had to do what she said. But I knew I'd lose it completely if I brought my foot down onto soft, dead flesh.

"The clock's ticking," she said.

It was now or never. I'd come much too far to stop now. I'd been mugged, knocked unconscious and searched, and I'd almost lost one of my favorite ties. I strongly suspected that if I didn't do exactly as this strange voice commanded, I'd be dead before the night ended.

Taking a deep breath, I brought my right leg up. Then, visualizing it moving a couple of feet forward, I brought it back down onto the hard, uneven surface of the floor. My heart raced as I repeated the procedure with my other leg. Luckily, I managed to do it without stepping on the corpse stretched out in front of me.

33

But I didn't have time to celebrate. The moment my left foot came down, the voice said, "Walk ten steps, turn left, then walk another ten steps. This will bring you back out to the street."

Once again, I obeyed her instructions. I counted ten paces and stopped cold. The moment I turned to my left, an open doorway appeared straight ahead, at the end of the hall. The intermittent flash of headlights piercing the darkness made my heart skip a beat. Freedom awaited me just a dozen or so yards straight ahead.

My first instinct was to run. I knew that would be a mistake. I still couldn't see the floor at my feet. To make this even more dangerous, this ordeal had drained me, and I could feel the exhaustion inching heavily up my legs to take over the moment I let down my guard. I'd been running on fear and adrenaline for the last hour or so and was terrified that my energy supply was about to run out. I didn't want to be anywhere near this area when it finally did. So I dug in with whatever I had left and kept up my cautious pace until I cleared the open doorway of the condemned building. I didn't hesitate even after I'd gone down the crumbling stone steps leading to the sidewalk.

Even though I felt totally free for the first time since I'd been knocked unconscious, I maintained my frantic pace, forcing my cramped legs and frozen feet to keep up the action until I reached my goal.

A lamp post at the corner splashed the cold, dismal night with an orange haze. The street directly straight ahead looked vaguely familiar, and as I struggled to increase my pace, I realized I'd come back out onto Liberty Avenue. Gino's Bar & Grill awaited me. I took off in that direction and didn't hesitate for even a moment.

By the time I reached the end of the block, I could feel the exhaustion taking over. My legs seemed to be wrapped in a heavy cloak of numbness that crept upward, until my midsection—as well as my arms—grew heavier and heavier. I felt like I'd been submerged in a vat of chilled molasses. And since my feet were numb with cold, taking each step had become an agonizing chore. I didn't know if I'd be able to make it to Gino's before collapsing.

But just before the panic tried taking over again, a strange and wonderful sight awaited me halfway down the block.

The Challenger was sitting exactly where I'd left it. For some strange reason, the punks hadn't yet moved it.

But this couldn't help me at all. They'd taken my keys, my wallet, and my cell phone.

How could I possibly get in the car and drive away?

I decided to drop into Gino's and tell them what happened. While they called the cops, I could relax in a chair and wait for my circulation to return. Hopefully, my feet weren't frost-bitten. Just a few minutes thawing out in a warm place might be all they'd need to recover.

But just as I turned to climb the stone steps leading to the bar, I saw that their neon lights were dark. The place was closed.

Desperation ripped into me. I wanted to collapse to the pavement and lie there until I no longer felt anything.

But just then, I heard the young woman once again. "Get in the car."

As I turned, I hoped to see her this time. But as before, no one was there. "I can't," I told her. "They took my—"

"Get in."

Do as she says, my mind ordered me. She hadn't steered me wrong yet, had she? She'd got me away from those punks, hadn't she?

Most important of all, she'd brought me *here*…

I staggered over to the Challenger, circled the front, and opened the driver door. Then I slid in and felt my lower extremities instantly blending into the front seat. I'd never realized just how comfortable the front seat of a car could be until that very moment.

I sat back and let my head drop against the padded headrest. Then I closed my eyes and felt the exhaustion deepening. I sighed in total ecstasy as the warmth rushed right up to smother me. I knew I didn't have much time. I had to drive somewhere safe.

Forcing myself to sit forward and focus, I gazed at the dash.

The keys were nowhere in sight.

I could only stare numbly at the empty ignition and wonder what I could possibly do, where I could possibly go from here. It was extremely cold in the Challenger. Not quite as cold as outside, but in a few hours, there would be little difference. I couldn't just sit here until morning. I'd freeze to death.

But I had to do *some*thing…

What on earth could I possibly do?

"Are you…still here?" I asked in desperation.

"Of course I'm still here. I'm gonna stay with you until you're safe."

"I won't be safe much longer." I shivered as the cold caressed me, and I pulled up the collar of my overcoat to protect my ears and the back of my neck. "In a couple of hours, I'll be frozen stiff."

"I wouldn't have helped you get this far just to let you sit here all night and freeze to death, would I?" she asked.

"The keys…they're not here." It sounded lame, but nothing else seemed to matter. "I can't go anywhere if I can't start the car."

"Maybe you won't have to."

"Whatever you're thinking you can do…how can I possibly…"

I couldn't finish my statement. By the time I glanced at the rearview mirror and saw the flashing blue lights, the exhaustion had moved farther up, settling in my head.

Darkness overtook me.

Numbness came next.

CHAPTER FOUR

When I opened my eyes, I discovered that I was lying in a strange bed.

I raised my head a few inches and cringed at the throbbing in the back of my skull. I lay back down and waited until it subsided. It seemed to take forever, but after a few minutes, it finally settled down. Taking a breath, I carefully raised my head again and scanned the room.

I was in a hospital. The room was small and monotonously white. A white cabinet stacked with boxes of gauze and cotton—as well as scissors and tweezers—sat along the white wall on my right. A white curtain spanned the center of the room on my left, just a foot or so from the edge of the bed. A tall, thickset woman dressed in white stood near the foot of the bed, scribbling something on a clipboard. Once she'd finished, she let the clipboard hang from the metal frame. Then she glanced at me.

"We were wondering when you'd finally decide to come back and join us," she said in a soft, low-pitched voice. "You haven't budged in twelve hours."

Twelve hours. I couldn't believe it. For a moment I thought she was kidding, but I knew better. I just couldn't believe that I'd been out cold for that long. "I've been asleep…for twelve *hours*?"

"That's the rumor."

"Twelve *hours*?" That fact alone staggered my imagination.

She smiled. "Lemme guess. You've got somewhere else to be?"

I ignored her comment. There were too many other things I wanted to know. "How'd I get here?" Right now, that was the most important issue.

She shrugged. "Most likely, in an ambulance."

I wasn't exactly in the mood for quips. "I *meant*—"

"Sorry, just a little hospital humor I thought I'd throw in. I honestly don't know. My shift just started two hours ago. I wasn't given the details— just that you'd suffered a nasty blow to the back of your head, as well as some other minor injuries. You've also suffered a slight concussion and early stages of frostbite on your toes, but all that's been taken care of."

Startled, I sat up and stared down at the foot of my bed. I tried wiggling them. They hurt at first and seemed stiff. "You didn't...I still *have* them, don't I?"

She smiled. "Amputation wasn't necessary. But your clothes weren't so lucky." She wrinkled her nose. "That suit looks pretty bad and smells like you took it much too close to a dump."

The jacket and trousers were draped more or less neatly over the back of the chair next to the foot of the bed, on my left. The jacket was dirty and stained in several places. The suit had cost me two grand, but I was much too grateful to be alive than be angry over damaged clothes. "Yeah, I did end up on the wrong side of the tracks. But in my defense, it really wasn't my idea."

She regarded it and shook her head. "A real shame. It's a nice suit, too."

"Then you have no idea who brought me in?" I really wanted to move on and find out what exactly had happened.

"I'm assuming the paramedics admitted you. Judging by your chart, a call was made yesterday morning, around three-thirty. You were brought in just before three-forty-five."

"And that's all you know?"

"The other nurses will know more, but yes, that's about it for me."

A vague image of Gino's Bar & Grill on Liberty Avenue flashed in my head. "I take it you have no idea where I was found?"

"Sorry." She turned to leave and then thought better of it. "By the way, there's a woman out in the waiting room who wants to talk to you."

"A woman?" My pulse hastened. Could it be the woman who'd saved my life? The lady who belonged to the voice that had guided me away from those street punks?

The nurse nodded. "A woman. Just like me, only younger, taller and prettier…with a *lot* more hair."

My imagination immediately went berserk. I could hardly contain myself.

"She said her name was Brittany Sanderson and that she works at E&S SoftSystems."

My heart sank. It wasn't the voice at all. But at least I knew what she was talking about. "She must be my contact."

"Ash-blond hair? A figure to die for?"

40

"I've never seen the lady before."

"Well, you're in for a treat."

"Actually, I came here for a business meeting. I have no control over who they've sent to pick me up." I found that I was a little irritated. I didn't know if it was because of her innuendoes or because I was frustrated that I couldn't find out anything about the voice.

"Well, she's a real looker."

"They must have heard what happened and sent her here to see how I'm doing."

"Would you like to see her?"

"Please."

"I'll have her come in. I guess I can let you two have fifteen minutes."

"Thank you."

She smiled and left the room.

I lay back and gritted my teeth as another seething wave of nauseating pain pounded the back of my skull.

I still couldn't believe I'd been lying here for twelve hours. It felt like such a very short time since I'd blacked out in the Challenger. But I didn't think the nurse would lie to me. It had no doubt taken some time to bring me here, examine me, fix the gash on the back of my head, and tend to my frozen toes and my other injuries.

Suddenly curious, I reached up and gingerly felt the back of my head. It was covered with a large bandage, and the effort had caused a sharp pain slicing down my back. I let my arm drop and sighed.

Then I tried remembering everything.

Doing a rough calculation, I figured that if I'd left Gino's at around eight-thirty, I was at the mercy of those street punks for at least six hours. I had no idea exactly how long I'd been unconscious, but they'd obviously had more than enough time to knock me unconscious, drag me into the alley, dump me on the cold, rough pavement, go through my pockets, and enjoy their evening meal.

And if I hadn't gotten away from them...

But I had. I had gotten away. I'd also managed to make it back to the rental...in one piece.

The voice was responsible. Somehow, the disembodied voice of a young woman had helped me escape certain death. I was convinced that if I hadn't heard the voice, I would surely have been murdered long before now.

I thought more about the voice and struggled to recall every detail.

Was it my imagination?

If not, what happened?

Was it really someone's voice? Or had the sharp blow to the back of my head injured a crucial part of my brain?

What if it *wasn't* my imagination? What if it *was* an actual voice?

Did it belong to someone I knew? Someone I didn't know?

Why couldn't I see her?

Just as total confusion settled in, so did the thought of what the voice had done. This woman— whoever she was—had somehow distracted them and gotten them away from me. Then she came back and guided me out of the alley, to the safety of my rental.

But who the hell *was* she?

How in heaven's name could I even begin to thank her when I didn't even know if she was real? How could I find out if she was real if no one else knew anything about—

"Mr. Danner? I'm Brittany Sanderson. I've been sent by E&S to make sure you've got everything you need and that you're being well taken care of…" She sent over a sort of embarrassed smile.

The nurse had been right in her appraisal. This woman was truly a babe. She appeared to be in her mid-thirties and was close to six feet tall in her heels. She had one of those long-limbed, slender bodies that made her legs look like they went on forever. She wore a dark-blue business suit with a cream-colored blouse and carried a large black leather handbag with the strap resting on her left shoulder. She gave the appearance of a serious businesswoman, but her looks and her sweet lavender smell softened the overall picture.

"I'm pleased to meet you." I returned her smile. "And yes, they're taking good care of me."

"First of all, Mr. Erikson told me to tell you how deeply sorry we are that this happened in the first place."

"You're not responsible for this." I winced at the sharp pain in my head.

She took a step closer to the bed. "Are you okay? Should I get the nurse?"

"No. I'll be fine, thanks."

43

"Are you sure?" She looked worried.

"I'm okay."

She waited a few moments, possibly to see if I'd pass out. When she decided it was all right to go on, she said, "Well, we still would like you to know how badly we feel about this. Mr. Erikson has already been in contact with the police and was assured that the matter will be handled as a top priority."

"That's very nice of you, but it was just a mugging, and—"

"It was inexcusable, and we'd like to make amends in whatever fashion we can. Mr. Erikson has already gotten with Mr. Crosley in Orlando and assured him that we'd take extra care of you."

"There was no need for you to do that…"

"It's just our way of trying to make this right. You're very important to us, and we'd like to continue dealing with your company for many years to come."

"I assure you that what happened to me will have nothing whatsoever to do with our future dealings."

She smiled. "I'm very pleased to hear that, but I still find it appalling that this happened."

I shrugged. "There really isn't much anyone can do about it now. I'm kind of pissed that a gang of street punks decided they wanted to relieve me of my wallet, cell phone and credit cards, but that sort of thing tends to happen these days. I guess I was in the wrong place at the wrong time. It wasn't your fault, and it certainly wasn't anything your company should be responsible for."

Mindful of my suit, she sat down in the chair and crossed her legs. I was right; they did seem to go on forever.

"It still shouldn't have happened at all," she said. "When we got a call from the police just a few hours ago—"

"From whom?" Suddenly reminded of the main issue, I realized once again that I needed to know exactly what happened. There had to have been some way the people at E&S were told about all this so quickly.

"The Police Department, of course."

"Obviously, but how would they know about you?"

She gazed at me in silence. I'd apparently said something she hadn't considered. "Well, they must've been told by someone that you'd been mugged, and—"

"What I mean is, how did the cops know to get in touch with you, specifically?"

She didn't reply. She obviously had no idea what I was talking about.

I decided to help her out. "No one else up here knows I'm here."

"No one at all?"

"I don't even know anyone here anymore. I haven't kept tabs on anyone from the old neighborhood for the last twenty years."

"You're not on Facebook?"

"Business takes up of most of my time nowadays. My boss and secretary know I'll be up here for two or three days, but other than that…"

"That's it, then."

45

"What's it?"

"Someone from Florida called and told them about your meeting."

"Who would do that? And how would they know what happened in the first place? I had no ID on me. Those punks robbed me. The paramedics had no idea who I am. Neither did the cops."

Her huge green eyes narrowed. "This *is* strange…"

"Ya think?"

"To say the least..."

"Then you tell me what *you* think happened."

She gazed at me in silence. I could tell she was trying to make sense of all this. "I have no idea what happened. None of this makes any sense at all. If you're right, and since those hooligans robbed you, then, yes, you had no ID on you anyone could use to figure out who you are. And since you were unconscious, the paramedics had no way of asking who you were or what happened."

"The cops might have lifted my prints when the paramedics were loading me into their van… But even if they did, how would they know to call you, specifically?"

"I don't know. I only know that you're safe now. Once I can get you out of here, I'll take you back to your hotel so you can rest. Mr. Erikson told me the meeting can be postponed for a couple of days so you can recover, if you wish."

"Did the hospital give you any idea when I'll be able to be released?"

"They said they need to do a few more tests to check and see just how severe your concussion was."

"Did they mention brain damage? Anything like that?"

"They wouldn't share that with me, but they did say they were optimistic about your condition."

"I guess that's hospitalese for saying I've got a hard head."

She smiled. Then she got up. "I'm gonna go out there and see if I can get a few questions answered. I'll be back as soon as I can."

"While you're out there, could I possibly borrow your cell phone? I've got to make a few calls to my credit card people and have them cancel my cards."

"Certainly." She rummaged through her bag, found her cell and handed it to me. "I'll be right back."

"I promise I won't go anywhere."

She was smiling as she left the room.

CHAPTER FIVE

Brittany came back about ten minutes later.

She sat down in the chair beside my bed and waited patiently until I'd finished with my last call.

About a minute later, my last transaction was completed. Suddenly tired, I gave Brittany back her cell and lay back on the pillow. "Did you find out anything?"

"A few things," she said.

"Really? I didn't think they'd confide in you."

"Neither did I. Since I'm not exactly family, they didn't want to share much at first, so I took one of the nurses aside and explained the situation."

"What did you tell her?"

"Well, I was told by Mr. Erikson that you're not married. This is true, isn't it?"

"Yes. Never married."

She blinked. "Never?"

"Nope."

"Problem?"

"Not at all."

"Then please go on."

"I also told her that we have no details about your immediate family, that we feel responsible for this unfortunate incident happening and would consider it a personal favor if we were told a couple of details so we might be able to communicate with the police to help them solve this case as quickly as possible."

"Are you the public relations guy for E&S?" I was really impressed. She was obviously the rare type of person who knew how to get things done.

She smiled. "I handle all sorts of things for them. And by the way, I'm a *gal*."

"It was just a figure of speech."

"Good thing. If I'm not, I've been spending *way* too much money on my gynecologist."

I laughed.

"You must be feeling better."

"It's the company. So tell me what else you found out."

"As I said, I found out a *few* things, but not nearly as much as I would have liked. The nurse was sympathetic. She told me someone called it in on the nine-one-one line and said you were the victim of a mugging and were lying unconscious in a Dodge Challenger on Liberty Avenue, about half a block east of Gino's Bar & Grill."

This was incredible. The moment I thought about that, I realized that this kind of information could have only come from someone who knew exactly what was going on...

And that meant, of course, the voice...

"This was probably why you were brought in so quickly," Brittany said.

"Anything on the caller?"

She shrugged. "I wouldn't know anything about that, Mr. Danner. All I learned was how the paramedics found out about you and how you were brought in so quickly..."

"Did the nurse happen to mention how *your* company was brought in on this?"

49

A pause. "I'm afraid that wasn't brought up, either..." She looked confused.

This was making less and less sense, and I realized once again that I knew just as little about all this as I did before. I decided to ask her a few specific details and see if I could glean anything at all from them.

"Okay...how did *you* find out about this?"

"You mean the emergency itself?"

"Yes."

"Mr. Erikson got a call."

"Did he tell you what the caller said?"

"Mr. Erikson said he was told by her that you'd been mugged and robbed. She also told him you were brought in to the hospital and—"

"*Her*. You said *her*. And *she*."

"Mr. Erikson said the caller was definitely a woman."

"Did she identify herself?"

"I don't recall him saying anything about that..."

"I thought the police and the hospital identified themselves when making such a call. And most 911 callers usually identify themselves as well."

"She probably mentioned the name of the hospital and then hung up."

"Probably?"

Brittany shrugged. "How else would Mr. Erikson know to tell me where to come?"

I didn't reply.

Brittany watched me in silence. I could tell something was on her mind. "Something's still bothering you, isn't it?" she asked.

"A couple of things."

"Care to share?"

"The woman who called and talked to your boss… She said what happened, when it happened, and where I was."

"Yes…"

"But she didn't say how she knew about *you*, did she?"

"You mean E&S?"

I nodded.

Brittany went silent. She seemed to be weighing all this in her head. Then she frowned. "No. As far as I know, she didn't."

***

After Brittany had left, the doctor and a different nurse came in to tell me they wanted me to stay until the next morning for further observation to determine if I should be discharged.

Since I was still exhausted and weak, the back of my head still aching, I wasn't too eager to get up and start moving around.

In other words, I didn't argue.

At around three that afternoon, a uniformed cop came in to ask me questions about the mugging. His nametag said *Randall*, and the three stripes on his sleeves told me he was a Police Sergeant. He was around forty, about six-two and beefy, with wide shoulders and huge hands. The moment he came in, he stopped at the foot of the bed and removed his service cap to expose a large skull shaved down to thick dark stubble. A two-inch jagged pink scar extended from the center of his lined forehead to the inside of his right eyebrow. He shoved his cap into

51

his left armpit and gave me a quick half-smile. "Mr. William Danner?"

"That's me."

He removed a thick leather-bound notepad from his jacket pocket and found a large black ballpoint pen in a different pocket. "I'm Sergeant Randall, and I'm with the Pittsburgh Police Department."

I wanted to tell him his blue uniform was a dead giveaway, but I didn't want to sound like a smartass. I just nodded and smiled politely.

"I was told you're from out of town."

"Winter Park, Florida."

"And I suppose you're visiting friends for the holidays?"

"Actually, I'm here to conduct business with E&S SoftSystems, a software brokerage on Smithfield."

"Is this your first visit to Pittsburgh?"

"I was born and raised here. I attended college at Carnegie-Mellon. I haven't been back in more than twenty years."

He raised both thick black brows. The scar on his forehead turned into a miniature lightning bolt. "Whereabouts are you from?"

"Gibsonia, actually."

He gave a brief hint of a smile. "Close enough. I'm from Richland Township."

"Small world."

He nodded and suddenly looked uncomfortable, shifting his weight while adjusting his collar. "Uh, sorry this happened. Can you give me some details about the perps that assaulted you?"

52

"There were four of them."

He began scribbling. "Any guess on their ages?"

"I'd say late teens."

"White? Black? Hispanic?"

"It was dark, but I'm reasonably sure they were white. At least, they *sounded* white. There might've been one Hispanic with them."

"They talk much?"

"Some. I caught their names, but they're probably just nicknames, or street names."

Another nod. "Lemme have 'em."

I tried hard to remember every detail. "One was called Jake. There was also a Chopstick, Naddie, and Jonesie. And I believe they mentioned someone they called Bugger. They were going to take my rental to him to have it chopped up."

He kept scribbling. "You pay attention to details. Great work. We know about Bugger and who he deals with, so at least we've got *some*thin'…"

"Any idea if this'll help catch those assholes?"

He stopped scribbling. "You've just given us a lot more than we knew before. It might not catch them or get your wallet and valuables back, but at least we've got enough details now to start building a case. By what you've just told me, I think we might have some idea where this gang hangs out, but street punks tend to move around, especially after a big score, so it'll be much harder to catch them. If I were you, I'd get with your credit card companies—"

"I already did. They're cancelled."

"Good deal. At least you've got that covered. Thieves usually try the ATMs right off to pull out as much cash as possible with the cards. If that doesn't work, they'll try selling them through a fence. We'll work from the ATM cameras and any other security monitors we can find in the area and then get with our local CI's to find out if they heard anything about stolen cards moving around during the last twenty-four or forty-eight hours. If we get a line on 'em, we'll grab 'em. Other than that?" He shrugged.

"I get it."

"Sorry, but that's the best we can do."

"Those are the breaks, I guess."

"I wish I could give you some hope, but…"

"I understand."

"At least you got away from the bastards. I was told out there that you're recovering nicely. Hopefully, you'll be okay when you leave here."

"E&S sent someone to take care of me."

"Great." He reached into his jacket pocket, pulled out a card and handed it to me. His name and number were printed on it. "Give me a call in a few days. I'll let you know what we've come up with. Will you be in town?"

"Since all this happened, I'll probably be here until after New Year's."

"Good deal. I hope the rest of your trip turns out well. And sorry about what happened." He put his cap back on, tipped it, then turned and marched out of the room.

***

Not long after Sergeant Randall had left, I discovered that I was tired.

Another nurse had brought in a tray of food, but after glancing at it and realizing just how unappetizing it looked, I pushed it aside. Then I lay back and began to reflect on the last twenty-four hours.

I wondered once again about the voice. Then it dawned on me that I hadn't heard it since I'd blacked out in the Challenger. Shouldn't I have heard it at least once after I'd regained consciousness? Shouldn't it have stuck around just long enough to give me the opportunity to thank it for saving my ass?

All of that made sense—at least, it did to me. But what if it wasn't meant to? What if it had all been a fluke? A weird malfunction of the mind brought on by the trauma of being struck on the back of the skull?

Maybe it hadn't really happened at all. Maybe it had been nothing more than my imagination…

Perhaps it really was brain damage. For all I knew, the sharp blow might have jarred something loose—something that had been able to fabricate the fantasy so realistically that I was totally convinced I was actually talking to some disembodied voice.

Considering this a medical issue, I worried that the blow might have been severe enough to blank out all logical thought. It might have even caused temporary madness, triggering some aspect of my subconscious I'd never even known about or had reason to use before.

I suddenly found that this thinking was making my head hurt.

Was all this really necessary?

Did I have to reason this predicament half to death to actually understand it?

Why did I have to understand it at all? It wasn't necessary, was it? The fact that it had happened should have been enough. I'd seen, heard, and read about enough strange things to conclude that everything in life didn't necessarily have to be explained or understood.

The simple fact was that I'd been mugged, hit over the head and dragged into an alley. I'd heard a voice. This voice—that of a woman—had helped me get away by maneuvering—in total darkness—down the hall in a condemned building, while four vicious young savages were a safe distance away, distracted by strange sounds they'd heard just as they were about to do me in...

This was where my imagination theory rapidly fell to pieces.

I'd never been in that alley before—how could I possibly know how to maneuver in a strange building—especially at night, and in total darkness? How would I know about the closet? The stuff gathered in its center? The sleeping bum in the hall? The hall itself?

How about the corpse lying in the hall farther down?

Was there actually a corpse lying there?

I couldn't see it, could I? I couldn't see the bum, either...

Was it all fabricated? Designed by my own paranoia to make it more realistic?

Even if it all had been fabricated, what about those strange sounds that came about at the most perfect moment? Were they part of the fantasy, too?

What about the street thugs? If they were part of the delusion, how did I get this lump on the back of my skull?

And what about my loss of consciousness in the Challenger? The fact that I'd been found, picked up and brought to the hospital?

How could I think for one instant that my imagination had been responsible for all that had happened?

And how could anyone possibly explain E&S being contacted once the paramedics were called?

As I thought about the whole thing, I concluded that it was real, and had really happened. And since it *had* happened and I *had* awoken in a hospital bed, the only person who could have contacted both 911 and E&S was the same person who knew what happened, where I was, and what was going on.

Someone who had seen it all.

Someone who'd been there with me...

And the only person, or presence, who had been there with me was the invisible young woman who'd guided me safely away from danger.

I suddenly realized that I was much more exhausted than I thought. My head still throbbed, and all this rationalizing was taking its toll. My eyelids grew heavy. The moment I let them close, I drifted off into a warm state of soft gray.

CHAPTER SIX

The gray thinned just moments later and gradually disappeared, revealing a familiar two-story red brick house and a row of well-tended bushes spanning its front.

Everything seemed hazy, almost like an old painting weathered by the elements and extreme age, but as I approached the house, the haze lifted, and the house and front yard grew much clearer.

It was the house where my Uncle John and Aunt Evelyn had lived for many years. It stood in the center of a block of similar homes in an old section of South Hills, where my parents and I went quite often while I was growing up.

Once the haze had disappeared, my cousin Johnny came outside. He was twelve again, as I was, and I realized when I glanced at the driveway and saw Dad's two-year-old shiny black Blazer parked there that we'd come for one of our weekend visits.

Johnny and I ran into the back yard and down the long hill, to explore the vacant property at the foot of the hill, where ten wooded acres separated their block from low-income tenement housing that went on for several blocks.

"Let's climb trees," Johnny said as we entered the woods.

"Sounds like fun." I stayed close beside him, and the two of us began pushing aside low-hanging branches and loose vines as we ventured farther into the heavy brush.

"You're in your good clothes." He was frowning at my outfit. My mother always made me wear my best jeans, a freshly-cleaned shirt and my favorite tennies whenever we went to visit relatives.

"I don't care. I wanna climb a tree!"

There were several tall enough to challenge two twelve-year-old boys willing to risk their lives and personal safety to brag about who could climb the highest. We chose two oaks at least forty feet in height and about fifty feet from one another.

It didn't take me long at all before I reached the top. I was much taller than Johnny and considerably stronger. My long arms didn't fail me when I jumped up to grab onto the lowest limb. I was also skinnier than my cousin, which helped in my ascent. From then on it was easy. I used the sturdy branches as steps, propelling myself upward while grabbing onto the limb above me for support and balance.

It only took me fifteen minutes to reach the top. When I could go no farther, I wrapped my arms and legs around its narrow trunk and held on even though my weight caused the top section to bend at a forty-five-degree angle. It didn't matter. I was a kid; I didn't care about broken bones, death, or disfigurement. If I'd fallen, I knew it would be no big deal. Casts were cool. You could get them signed by everyone, and it got you out of chores for weeks.

As I swayed dangerously just ten feet or so from the top, I saw that Johnny had only made it halfway up his tree. Just as he tried shinnying up to the next branch, his pant leg caught on something, and he stopped cold. The moment he tried twisting around to see how badly he was hung up, he slipped and lost his footing. He held on for dear life, until he finally lost his grip. Then he fell to the ground.

Luckily, his fall turned out to be just ten feet or so onto soft ground, but the branches had scraped and sliced his arms and stomach along the way, and he eventually had to admit defeat.

As he trudged back up the hill to face intense examination, medical treatment and harsh scolding by Aunt Evelyn, I climbed back down.

This was when I noticed someone watching me just beyond the clearing.

A girl a year or two younger than me was standing in front of the bushes about twenty feet away. She had heavy dark-brown hair and the largest dark-brown eyes I ever saw. She was short and scrawny, and wore a dirt-smudged gray tee shirt, scuffed jeans, and beat-up tennies. Her hair was thick and long and moved across her narrow shoulders when the afternoon breeze brushed against it.

She was smiling at me.

"Hi," I said. I hadn't liked girls much at that age but had recently discovered that I didn't mind them nearly so much anymore. This girl seemed pretty cool. Her hair was nice to look at, the way it shined when the sun hit it at a certain angle.

"You climb good." Her voice was low and kind of husky for her age.

I puffed up a little. "It was nothin'."

"You did better than Johnny."

I shrugged. "I don't get a chance to climb at my place. Not enough good trees in the neighborhood."

She nodded but didn't say anything.

I wondered how long she'd been watching us.

"I'm Jenna."

"I'm Bill."

I moved closer.

Then I saw that her left eye was discolored.

"How'd you get the black eye?"

She stopped smiling and pushed some hair in front of her face to cover her eye. "I fell."

"Really?"

"I gotta go." She spun around and scurried back through the woods. In just seconds she was gone.

Everything turned fuzzy again.

I opened my eyes and realized that I was still lying in the hospital bed.

My head had already resumed pounding again.

***

That night, just before the nurse came in to check on me, I found myself totally distracted by my memory of a little girl I once knew very briefly as a child.

I discovered that, for some strange reason, I'd been trying to remember every single detail about her. But as hard as I tried, I found my memory failing in every aspect.

Perhaps it was because I had no idea *why* I was thinking of her. Had I dreamed about her? If so, why? I'd only seen her two or three times during those few years and hadn't seen or heard anything about her since I grew up, left home, and began my professional career in Florida.

Why, after all these years, was I suddenly obsessed about a little girl I didn't even know?

My eyelids began to grow heavy. I could feel my body relaxing. Long before I realized it, I'd nodded off. For an instant I thought I caught a glimpse of a scrawny little girl with dark-brown hair standing a few feet from the bed, watching me. But just as her face grew clearer, I felt someone placing a cold hand over my wrist.

I snapped awake.

It was the nurse. She was smiling at me as she took my pulse. "Good dream?"

"What?" I was a little groggy and had no idea what she was talking about.

"You were smiling."

"Damn. I hate when that happens."

"You don't remember it?"

"You woke me up."

She looked concerned. "It must've been a doozy."

"Why do you say that?"

"Your pulse is over a hundred."

I sighed. "You probably did that when you woke me."

"I guess I scared you."

"Just a little."

"Sorry, but I've got to do my job."

"Scaring me?"

"You're funny."

I nodded and lay back.

While she checked my vitals, I tried remembering the dream. After about a minute or so, I realized it was no use. I had absolutely no recollection of what I'd been dreaming.

The nurse finally straightened and draped her stethoscope around her neck. "By the way, who's Jenna?"

"What?"

"You said, "Jenna," just before you woke up. Girlfriend?"

Jenna. The little dark-haired girl was named Jenna Caulfield. The mere mentioning of it should have started up a slew of memories, but I found that I remembered little else...

"Not really. Just a little girl I saw a couple of times growing up."

"That's odd."

"Howzat?"

She shrugged. "Having a great dream about a little girl you only saw a couple of times growing up. It just seems to me that there should be more to it."

"That lump on my head must've done more damage than we thought."

"I doubt it. According to your chart, you're recovering nicely. Your concussion was extremely mild." She took my pulse again. "It's settled down now. And so should you." She put her hand behind my head and gently raised it to adjust my pillow. "Let us know if you need anything. I'm just a button away."

"Thanks. If I've learned anything during the last twenty years, it's how to press a woman's buttons."

"Like I said, you're a real comedian." Shaking her head, she left without another word.

Sighing, I relaxed and stared up at the ceiling. In moments I drifted right off to sleep.

Then I had another dream.

My cousin Johnny and I were sitting on the patio out in back of his South Hills home when I saw Jenna again. It was the middle of summer, and school would begin in just a few weeks. She was dressed in shorts and a red-and-brown plaid shirt at least two sizes too large. She was peeking at us from behind an oak tree in the woods at the bottom of the hill.

I looked up from the video game we were playing. "That girl...you know her?"

"Yeah." Johnny didn't raise his eyes from our game.

"Her name's Jenna, right?"

Johnny scowled. "She's weird."

"She come here much?"

"I see her in the woods once in a while."

I watched her a little longer. Her knees were dirty, or all cut up. I couldn't see her face very clearly; her hair hid most of it. Besides, she was too far away. I remembered her black eye from when I'd last seen her and hoped it had healed all right. "She gets hurt a lot," I said.

"Her family's weird."

"Whaddya mean?"

"It's all messed up. Her stepdad drinks. Her mom left home a while ago. So did her brothers. I hardly ever see her in school."

It took me only a moment to understand what he'd just said. "Her stepdad beats her up?"

Johnny shrugged. "Who knows? You gonna play or what?"

I stared at him and wondered why he sounded so cold. He seemed concerned only about our game.

Then I turned back to where Jenna had been peeking at us. I raised my arm to wave.

She'd already disappeared.

CHAPTER SEVEN

Brittany Sanderson came to pick me up at the hospital at around eleven o'clock the next morning.

I was still a little weak, but the throbbing in my head had ebbed considerably, leaving me with just a slight headache.

A big guy with a shaved head and one thick black eyebrow helped me into a wheelchair. He wheeled me out of the room and into the area where I was to be discharged. Brittany waited patiently while I signed several insurance forms. Then I was wheeled down the hall and into the elevator, and we went down to the parking garage.

"I can walk, you know," I told the guy holding onto my wheelchair.

"Hospital policy, sir," he said flatly, sounding bored.

"Just take it easy," Brittany told me. "You'll be back in your hotel room in twenty minutes. Once we get there, you can walk around all you want."

Moments later, the hospital guy helped me into the passenger seat of Brittany's silver Lexus. I began feeling better once we got out of the parking garage. I could feel my limbs recovering and hoped that in a day or two, I'd be my old self again.

"Can we stop at a bank?" I asked. "I'll feel better once I can withdraw some money. I'm sort of destitute right now."

"Mr. Erikson already took care of that. He got with Mr. Crosley and two thousand dollars was wired into our personal account. I've got the money in my bag. I'll give it to you when we get to the Fairmont. I've also been instructed to draw out more—up to ten thousand—if you need it."

"That was awfully nice of you guys to do that."

"It was no trouble. As I've already said, we feel just awful about what happened."

"I hope you realize how much I appreciate you carting me around like this."

"It's the least we can do."

"Judging by how I'm feeling, I'll probably want to go ahead with the meeting a day or so after Christmas."

"You're sure about that?"

"I'm pretty confident I'll be feeling better and ready to go in two or three days."

"What are your plans for tomorrow?"

"I'll probably have dinner at the hotel and spend the evening quietly in my room with some wine. The room has a widescreen, so I'll be okay. I'm sure they'll be showing some decent movies."

"You don't mind being all alone? On Christmas?"

I shrugged. "It's not like I have much of a choice. The cops have my rental car; they'll probably keep it until they crack the case. I can't rent another car without sufficient IDs, and since those little idiots took my wallet…"

She sent over a half-smile, as well as a slight shrug. "*I'm* available…"

I didn't reply. A beautiful woman I didn't even know telling me she was available. This was every man's dream. I was at a loss for words.

She stopped at a light and watched me curiously. "Nothing to say? How about, thanks, Brittany, I appreciate the gesture?"

"You don't have plans for Christmas day?"

"Of course I do. I can cancel them."

"Why would you want to?"

"Well, like everyone else, I feel badly for what happened to you and want to do whatever I can to make amends."

"This wasn't your fault, you know."

"It still happened, didn't it? No reason why we shouldn't at least try and make things a little better for you. It *is* Christmas, you know."

"Honestly, I don't know what to say. Are you sure you don't mind?"

"It's really no big deal. I was supposed to spend Christmas with my family, but since this came up, I decided to put the company first."

"Where's your family?"

"North Hills."

"How often do you see them?"

"Just about every week. They'd like it much better if it was every *day*, and I'm sure they'd really love it if I lived across the street…or moved back into my old bedroom. But they've learned to deal with my independence. I *am* over thirty, after all. It seems like I need to remind them of that almost constantly."

"You have brothers or sisters?"

"Both. Why?"

"Just curious."

"So? Do you want to spend Christmas with me?"

68

"Do you usually do this for visiting clients?"

"No..."

"Then why *are* you doing it?"

"Is that a yes? Or a no?"

"It's a yes, but—"

"All right, then. I'll come over tomorrow morning and pick you up. When will you be ready to leave?"

"I usually get up around eight o'clock on my off-days. Tomorrow I'll probably sleep in, so I most likely won't want to get out of bed until nine."

"I'll pick you up at ten. Will that be all right?"

"That'll be fine."

The light changed; we started moving again.

"Would you mind making a stop on the way to the hotel?" I asked.

"Not at all. Where?"

"The closest state store. I'm gonna need some port wine to help me relax this evening."

"No problem."

***

The state store on Penn Avenue buzzed with people stocking up for their holiday cheer.

I grabbed a bottle of Taylor Port while Brittany picked up a small bottle of Benedictine Brandy. While we waited at the end of the long line at the counter, I tried focusing on things other than my aching joints and back, as well as the pain in the back of my head. At least I was able to lean against the counter to ease some of the pressure off my spine. The prospect of having Christmas dinner with this beautiful lady also lifted my spirits.

"How excited were you—I mean really—about having Christmas dinner with your family?" I asked.

"We've been doing the usual family get-together thing with the folks and relatives ever since I can remember. Why?"

"I can't help feeling guilty for keeping you away from them…"

"Please don't. I'll probably have New Year's dinner with them, so…well, just don't, okay?"

I could tell she wasn't lying to me, so I just smiled. "Any thoughts about where you'd like to have dinner?"

"I thought we'd be better off if I just fixed something at my place. The restaurants here are murder on Christmas Day."

"As I recall, nearly half of them are closed. The really good ones that are open are booked solid."

"It hasn't changed much at all."

Suddenly I had an idea. "How about the Fairmont? I was only there long enough to drop off my bags, but it's a really swanky place. I saw a bunch of ads for dinner the Habitat's having tomorrow. It sounds like they're going all out. It could be really great."

She tilted her head. "Mr. Danner, could this be your subtle way of rescuing me from rushing around, fighting the crowds—and the horrible traffic—to do some last-minute grocery-shopping on Christmas Eve?"

"Damned straight. And since we'll be spending so much time together, please call me Bill. All my friends do—that is, if I had any."

She laughed.

"What part of that did you find amusing?"

She shrugged. "I can't believe a really nice, personable guy like you doesn't have any friends…"

"Thanks for the compliment, but I don't. Not really."

"You can't be serious. I haven't heard a bad word about you. Not from Mr. Erikson or anyone else at E&S who's ever dealt with you."

"Well, I've always found it best to treat people how I'd like to be treated. It's not only easier, it also causes less problems. But I'm serious about having no friends. I've always preferred keeping to myself. You never have to explain your actions or motivations to yourself. And if you do, you might want to look into finding a reputable therapist to talk to."

She smiled. "I believe you. But getting back to the issue… You're beginning to sound like someone who's never been married."

"Guilty."

Her green eyes grew. It made me wonder if she thought I was lying again. "Really?"

"You find it that hard to swallow?"

"I guess not. Marriage isn't that important nowadays. You've had girlfriends, haven't you?"

"Of *course* I've had girlfriends. Tons of them. What about you?"

She smiled. "Sorry. No girlfriends."

I laughed. "I guess I deserved that one, didn't I?"

"I was just kidding."

71

I nodded. "On a serious note…are you married?"

"Used to be. We divorced about a year ago, after five years."

"Was it bad?"

She gave me a half-smile. "I'm still coping, but I'm fine."

I could see the light draining from her face and decided it was time to change the subject. "So then…what about the Fairmont thing?"

"Well, it does sound inviting…"

"Is it a date, then?"

"I have to drive over tomorrow anyway, so…"

"Why?"

"I kind of volunteered to chauffer you around. Since you don't have a car, you'll be forced to take cabs, and that would really be a bummer, especially after what you went through..."

"Why *did* you volunteer?"

She shrugged. "I'm usually the one who always volunteers for the dirty jobs."

I couldn't help smiling. "Now I'm a dirty job… How unpleasant. And offensive. And tacky. I'm hurt. And slighted."

She laughed. "I didn't mean it *that* way…"

"I was just pulling your wire."

"I just meant that whenever something comes along no one else has time for—"

"They call you Dirty Brittany at the office?"

Her green eyes narrowed. "Don't be silly…"

"By the way, you never said where you live."

"North Hills."

"How far from your folks?"

72

"Not far enough. About three miles."

"Not far enough?" I could tell I'd hit a nerve.

She sighed tiredly, as if she'd been through this too many times before. "It gets a little inconvenient once in a while—especially when they decide to come over without calling or call and ask me to come right over. And when I ask why, they always say it's extremely important. And when I jump in the Lexus and rush over, it's usually for something stupid, like the two of them having a tiff, and Mom wanting some of the family at the table besides Dad. But they're my parents, so…" She shrugged.

"Mine separated years ago. I never see them anymore."

"I'm sorry. I didn't mean to sound so…well, so callous…"

"I know. It's a double-edged sword. You either have them and want to shoot them, or you don't have them and wish you still had them around."

"One time, my father came over when I was having dinner with a prospective date…"

"I'll bet *that* was interesting." I could well imagine such an image.

"Thank God it was just dinner. The man was a client, and we decided to have dinner at my place before I drove him back to the airport so he could fly back to New York."

We were just two customers away from the cashier when I felt someone's eyes on me. When I turned toward the door, I thought I saw a scrawny little girl with thick dark-brown hair standing beside the door, watching me.

Was it—

73

No. It *couldn't* be.

Suddenly dizzy, I put the bottle of port on the counter and rubbed my eyes.

"Are you all right?" Brittany looked worried.

The dizziness ebbed slightly as I waited for my vision to clear.

"Bill?" Brittany placed a hand on my arm. "Everything okay?"

"I'm fine." My vision cleared. I turned back toward the entrance.

The little girl had vanished.

CHAPTER EIGHT

Unnerved by what happened in the state store, I chose not to let it ruin the rest of our day.

Brittany hadn't said much about the incident on the way over from Penn Avenue. She'd glanced at me several times as she drove but asked me only once if I was feeling all right. I could tell she was being tactful and knew she was somewhat suspicious. I couldn't blame her. I'd probably feel the same way under the same circumstances.

Even so, I had no intention of telling her that I'd just seen what I could only describe as a hallucination, and that it looked very much like the little girl I'd dreamed about at the hospital. I'd just met Brittany and already liked her very much. I could tell she was growing to like me as well. I didn't want to scare her off so quickly by demonstrating to her that I might be mental.

But I couldn't help wondering why I kept seeing this same little girl. Part of me was totally convinced that this hallucination was Jenna, who I'd seen only a couple of times as a kid. However, the other part—that portion of my brain that clung stubbornly to logic and scoffed at things like hallucinations and figments of my imagination—suggested that this might have had something to do with the blow to the head I'd sustained just two days earlier.

This, of course, brought me right back to the voice that had saved me and sent the paramedics directly to me. Even my logic couldn't prevent me from putting those two facts together.

But what did my memories of Jenna have to do with the voice in the alley? The voice I'd heard was that of a young woman—not a child.

Were the two connected?

If so, how?

Most importantly, why did I keep seeing Jenna?

"Where *are* you?" Brittany asked as she turned at the light and followed the long line of traffic onto Market Street.

"I'm right here." I realized only then that I must have zoned out again. Then I cursed myself for acting so foolish. I was sitting beside a beautiful woman, but instead of enjoying the moment, I continued fantasizing over the hallucination of a young girl I hadn't seen in thirty years.

I really am mental, I told myself. *I really do need psychiatric help.*

"You seem somewhere else," she said.

"I guess I'm just tired. The last few days…" I shook my head.

She nodded. "Sorry. I should be more sympathetic."

"You're not doing anything wrong, believe me. This is all on me. I need to focus on the here and now and forget about what happened two nights ago."

We reached the Fairmont Hotel shortly after one-thirty.

The pine-scented lobby was handsomely decorated with hanging garlands, ribbons and bows, and dozens of ornaments placed tastefully in the

76

windows, on the front desk, and on the polished furniture. A huge, lavishly decorated pine tree dominated the sitting area; large sprigs of holly and clusters of old-fashioned Christmas balls and stars hung from the chandeliers.

The decorations and cheerful feel of our new surroundings lifted my spirits immediately. A lavish sign on an easel next to the hall that led to the Habitat listed their Christmas Eve specials. The moment I saw roast beef with sautéed mushrooms and onions, asparagus, wild rice, and a variety of pies and cheesecakes available from the dessert bar, I realized just how hungry I was. I hadn't eaten much at all at the hospital; their food had been unappetizing and tasteless. Aside from the mint jell-O and their chocolate custards, what food I'd managed to force down hadn't been enough to keep an infant alive.

"Are you hungry?" I asked.

"Actually, I'm *starving*." Her eyes stayed fixed on the menu as well. "All I had for breakfast was a stale croissant and a cup of coffee."

I held out my arm. "My treat? I have even money—thanks to you."

She took it and laughed. "I graciously accept the offer, kind sir."

***

The meal was delicious, the roast beef to die for.

The service was impeccable. The Christmas carols piped in through the speaker system gave the occasion an especially festive feel.

77

During the meal, Brittany and I exchanged more small talk. I learned that she was the youngest in her family, with two brothers and two sisters. One sister lived in Richland Township and worked as a doctor's assistant with her husband, a pediatrician. The other sister worked as a paralegal secretary at a law firm on Penn Avenue. Her two brothers also lived fairly close—one in Butler, the other in Pleasant Hills. They were in their early forties, both executives with investment companies. Her father had retired from the Air Force three years earlier. While he repaired furniture for relatives and neighbors in their two-car garage, her mother maintained their spacious North Hills home.

It was obviously a close-knit family, one very similar to what mine had been before my parents began having serious problems just a year or so before I graduated from high school.

Soon we were enjoying the Habitat's excellent cheesecake selections. I chose vanilla, Brittany chocolate, and it wasn't long before we both realized we'd eaten too much. However, the pain in the back of my head had all but vanished, and I actually felt revitalized. The meal and the pleasant company had been just what I'd needed. I sat back and had a sip of my wine.

Then, just as Brittany began talking about the food and the quality of service, I caught movement in the corner of my eye. I turned. Our waitress was approaching our table, our bill on a silver tray in her hand.

For an instant I thought I saw the little dark-haired girl following her.

Dizziness enveloped me, and I imagined I saw the table—as well as the floor—shifting in front of me. But even as I fought the sudden vertigo, I knew something wasn't quite right; the plates weren't sliding off the table. I was just about to grab the table for balance when I heard a soft voice close to me.

"Bill?" It was Brittany. "You all right?"

My vision cleared. The waitress was walking away, heading back to the kitchen. Brittany was standing over me. She looked worried as she gently shook me.

My God, I thought, the cold fear shooting through me. *It's happened again...*

"Bill?"

Forcing myself to snap out of it, I forced a weak smile in her direction. "Sorry about that." I sincerely hoped downplaying this might work better than filling her in on what seemed to be the continuation of my complete mental breakdown.

"Did you zone out or something? You had a really weird expression on your face."

"I'm afraid I'm still suffering intermittent periods of dizziness. The knot on the back of my skull…it apparently did more damage than I thought. I'm afraid it's affected my equilibrium." I reached up and gingerly felt the fresh bandage the nurse had replaced just before I'd left the hospital. The wound was a little tender—hardly worth worrying about anymore—but I made the gesture just for show. I didn't want Brittany to think anything else was going on.

"Did they give you any meds for it?"

"They gave me two Tylenol, but I left them on the table. Tylenol always makes me nauseous. I was going to buy some Ibuprofen whenever I can find my way to a drugstore."

"I think I might have some of those in my bag…" She snatched the bag from the chair, placed it in her lap and opened it.

"It's all right. I feel much better already."

"It's no problem." She rummaged through the bag, found a small vial, opened it, and dropped two in her palm. She handed them to me. "I'll feel better if you take them. I know how awful headaches can be."

I took them from her. "I really don't want to take them now because I've had so much wine, but I promise I'll take them later, before I go to bed. All right?"

"Of course. I'm sure they'll help."

"And thank you." I wrapped them in a napkin and shoved them down my pants pocket. "I appreciate it."

"It's no bother at all." She had another small sip of her wine. "You're sure you feel all right now?"

"I'm fine. In fact, I feel good enough to see what they're doing on Market Street. They used to put on quite a display at Christmas Eve when I lived here years ago. Do they still do it?"

"As far as I know."

"Would you like to see what they're doing? We can brave the cold for half an hour or so, can't we?"

Brittany smiled. "That sounds like fun."

***

Market Street exploded with twinkling lights and loud, enthusiastic carolers.

The surrounding buildings, all lit up in red, green, and gold, bathed the busy area in a brilliant happy glow. A large tree glittering with lights lit up the center of the Square. Small crowds, oblivious of the cold and the hint of snow in the air, strolled down the walk.

Brittany and I went over to one of the dozen or so concession stands lining the street and bought two large cups of hot cocoa. As we sipped the delicious, steaming brew, we went over to one of the few vacant park benches. For the next few minutes, we watched the slow-moving crowd while a growing number of carolers gathered around the tree, chanting "Little Drummer Boy."

"This is really nice," Brittany said. "It really puts you in the Christmas spirit."

I could tell by her gleaming smile that she was having a good time.

"It really does," I agreed. "If I hadn't been mugged and nearly killed, you would have missed out on all this."

She laughed. "That's one way of looking at it, I guess…"

"A wise man always sees the good in everything that happens in life."

"Is that a quote from someone?" she asked.

"I have no idea. I figured I just thunk up that one on my own."

She smiled. "We'll go with that, then."

"Agreed." I had another sip of hot cocoa.

Brittany sat up. "Would you like to mosey on over to the tree and check out the ornaments?"

"Actually, I'm a little too comfortable right now to do any worthwhile moseying."

"Would you mind if I went over and checked it out? I'll only be a moment."

"Not at all."

"You're sure?"

"Go ahead, enjoy yourself. I'll be here when you get back."

"I hope so. I'd hate to think I could scare you off so quickly."

"A guy would have to be blind, gay, or totally insane to be scared off by a lady like you."

She was smiling, but I could tell she was trying to decide if I was serious. "I may be totally wrong, but that certainly sounded like one really terrific compliment…"

"It was when I said it. I was afraid it wouldn't come out quite right."

The green eyes stayed focused on mine. "It came out just fine."

"Good. I'm glad something's finally going right for me."

"Do you want my advice?"

"I probably could use it."

She smiled. "Keep up the good work."

It brought a smile to my lips and made me feel much better.

She stood up. Before moving away, she watched me for a few moments. "You promise you won't zone out again while I'm gone?"

"I can't guarantee it, but as I told you before, I feel fine."

"All right, then. I'll only be a minute or so. And please don't go anywhere, okay?"

I bowed. "As you say, milady…"

She gave me one last smile. Then she turned and went down the narrow walk that led to the Christmas tree.

The moment I was alone, I heard someone approaching me.

I turned. It was the dark-haired little girl.

My heart skipped a beat, and I could barely find my voice. "This may sound weird, but you look just like a little girl I used to know a long time ago, when I was just a kid."

She didn't reply. Without a word, she stepped closer, reached up and touched my shoulder.

A warm tingling ran down my body.

In the next instant, blackness consumed me.

CHAPTER NINE

The blackness cleared a moment later, and I found that I was standing at the foot of the hill behind my cousin Johnny's two-story red brick house in South Hills.

It was no longer winter. It was quite warm, and the approaching darkness suggested that it was nearly well past seven at night.

What the hell was going on? Why was I here?

More importantly, how did I *get* here?

Just moments ago, I was sitting on a park bench with Brittany Sanderson in Market Square in downtown Pittsburgh. It was Christmas Eve. We'd just had a remarkable dinner at the Habitat in the Fairmont Hotel and decided to enjoy a cup of hot cocoa while watching the joyous holiday activity down the street. I was getting to know a lovely young woman and was having more fun than I'd had in a long time.

But in the mere blinking of an eye, something strange happened. The little dark-haired girl I'd been seeing and dreaming about the last couple of days had suddenly come over to the bench I was sitting on and changed everything with a mere touch of her hand. My hot cocoa was gone. So was Brittany. Market Square also vanished, and with it, the cold evening, the carolers, the glittering lights, Christmas Eve, and Pittsburgh itself.

Now, for some reason I could not comprehend, I was standing here in my cousin's back yard, miles away from the city, all alone and—

No. I *wasn't* alone.

The little dark-haired girl had come here with me. Her name was Jenna, and I'd seen and talked to her no more than two or three times in my youth. She stood just a couple of feet from me, and even though I was totally convinced she was a hallucination, she looked very real standing there, watching me in the same fashion as she'd watched me all those many years ago, when we were both very young and had our entire lives ahead of us…

That was another strange thing about all this. Back then, we were both just a couple of years apart. But right now I was the same forty-two that I'd been the last three or four months—a grown, mature adult male slightly past his middle years… However, Jenna hadn't changed at all. She was still ten or eleven years old…

"Jenna?"

She nodded.

"You're still here."

Another nod.

"That was you back there? At the park bench?"

"That was me."

Something was very, very wrong. Worse, it was making no sense.

"And you're still…the same age you were when I…when I saw you last…"

She smiled.

"How can that be?"

No reply.

"What's going on?"

A shrug.

"Jenna, *please* tell me what's going on. Why am I here?"

"I brought you here."

"Yes. I kind of figured that one out all by myself. But why? How is all this possible?"

"I wanted you to come back. I wanted you to come back and see me…one more time."

What did that mean? And why did it sound so *final*?

"But why here? Why now?"

"This is where it all began."

"Where all *what* began? Jenna, please *talk* to me. Explain this to me."

"I will. In time, I'll tell you everything."

"In time?"

She nodded but said nothing else.

I scanned the area. It only took me a few moments to discover that nothing had changed. More than twenty-five years had gone by since I'd been here last, but this place looked the same. Even though I'd heard over the years from my cousin and from several other sources that the woods had been cleared years ago to make room for a development of condominiums and town houses, the woods remained unchanged and completely unaffected by the years. Johnny's house hadn't changed at all.

The same swing stood just twenty feet or so from Aunt Evelyn's rock garden in the back yard, where it had been since Johnny and I were seven or eight. The swing didn't look any older, nor had it been affected even in the slightest by rust or by the elements. The French doors leading to the game room still looked just as new as they did when

Uncle John had them installed when Johnny and I were both around eight or nine. I expected to see definite signs of age—or at least some wear—on the roof. However, the shingles hadn't aged a single day.

The cars parked in the driveways of the other houses on the block even looked the same.

It was almost as if time had stood completely still...

"Jenna, what did you do?"

"Like I just said, I wanted to bring you back."

"Back where?"

"Back here."

"But why?"

"I needed to."

"Again, why?"

"I have to tell you a few things."

"Jenna, you can tell me something right now."

She nodded.

"Why are you still a little girl?"

She smiled. "You'll see."

"What will I see?"

"Everything."

I scanned the area again. Everything had a soft, dreamlike quality to it...yet it all felt so incredibly real that I couldn't call any of it a dream.

"Jenna, please tell me how you were able to bring me here...and why it looks like we've gone back in time...and why you're still the same little girl I remember when I was twelve years old..."

Without a word, she held out her hand.

I just stared at it.

She wiggled her fingers, beckoning me to grasp her hand.

I ignored it. "Jenna, the last time you touched me, something strange happened."

"Take my hand, Bill."

"I honestly don't think I should…"

"Please?"

Her innocence—as well as the sincerity emanating from her—made me melt. I knew right then that she hadn't done all this—whatever all this actually was—to hurt me. I sighed and did as she asked.

The moment our hands touched, another wave of darkness enveloped me again.

CHAPTER TEN

The darkness vanished instantly.

Jenna and I were standing outside one of the tenement complexes on the other side of the woods. It was the late afternoon. Judging by the warmth and humidity, I guessed that it was late summer. Kids were running up and down the sidewalk behind us but didn't pay any attention to us. I suspected that they couldn't see us.

Once again, my curiosity—as well as my fear—began taking over, and I found that I was more than slightly shaken by all this.

"Jenna, what are we doing here? How'd we get here? What *is* all this?"

"*Sshhh*!" She let go of my hand, brought it up and pressed her index finger against my lips. I felt its warmth, its firmness. Right then I realized this *wasn't* a dream. It was real.

She finally pulled it away and pointed to the window just a couple of feet from us.

Inside the dimly lit room, a big, burly man around forty-five sprawled in an armchair, drinking beer and watching television. He was dark and balding and hadn't shaved in several days. He wore a stained white sleeveless tee shirt, loose-fitting jeans, and open-toed sandals, and scratched his ample belly as he slurped beer from a can and stared at the TV screen. When he finished the beer, he crushed the can and tossed it on the stained carpet. It joined the group of six others near the cluttered cocktail table. Then he turned toward the archway on his left and yelled, "More beer!"

Moments later, Jenna came in through the archway carrying a can of beer. Keeping her distance, she held it out to him. He snatched it from her so roughly that it nearly knocked her off-balance. He cracked open the can. Some of it bubbled up, the froth sliding down the side of the can and gathering thickly on the back of his hand. He wiped the spill on his pant leg. "What took ya so goddamn long?" Then, as she turned to leave, he reached out and swatted her on the back of the head, knocking her down.

Without a word, she got back up and scurried out of the room.

I found this extremely difficult to watch. "Jenna, why are you making me—"

Once again, she said, "*Sshhh!*" But this time, instead of shushing me, she shushed herself, and when she turned to look up at me, there were tears filling her large brown eyes.

The man in the chair finished his beer. He tossed the crushed can on the floor with the others and belched loudly. Then he yelled, "C'mere, bitch!"

Nothing.

He squirmed out of the chair and staggered closer to the archway. "Better get your scrawny ass here, you stupid little snot!"

Still nothing.

"If I have to hunt ya down, you're gonna wish you were dead!"

Head down, Jenna appeared stiffly in the hall.

"Where's my dinner?"

A shrug.

"I asked ya a question, ya little moron!"

Sighing, Jenna raised slowly her head and looked him straight in the eye. The moment her face came up, he slapped her viciously across the face, knocking her to her knees.

"I ain't gonna ask ya again, bitch!"

He took a step toward her. She scrambled to her feet and scurried out of the apartment.

"Get your mangy ass back here, goddammit! I ain't through with ya! And I want my dinner!"

I had to force myself to keep from turning away from the window. The tiny hand holding mine had grown cold and began trembling. It gripped mine with so much force that it cut off my circulation. Just as I turned to gaze at the terrified little girl beside me, she looked up at me with tear-stained eyes and sniffed.

"Was it just the two of you?" I asked softly.

"My brothers had already left home by that time. It was just me and my older sister…for a little while…"

"What happened to her?"

Another sniff. "Pauline died right after Momma left. Pneumonia."

"How long were you…how long did you…" I had no idea how to ask her how long she'd been forced to live like this.

Before I could get my question sorted out, she put her other hand over mine. Darkness fell over us again.

When it cleared, we were back at the foot of the hill behind Johnny's house, watching two young boys walking into the woods. One of them was my cousin; the other, of course, was me.

Jenna and I watched closely as Johnny and my other image climbed the two large oaks. Her hand still gripped mine, but not nearly so tightly. She no longer trembled. I turned to gaze at her face. She was smiling brightly; her tears had gone.

Just then, Johnny slipped on his branch and began sliding back down.

Jenna laughed. She turned to me. "I was really glad you won."

"Why?"

"I never liked Johnny."

"Why not? He was an okay guy."

Her smile vanished and she frowned. "He treated me…like everyone else."

I knew better than ask her anything else. I remembered how he'd dismissed her when I'd first asked about her.

As Johnny trudged back up the hill, favoring his skinned side, arms and legs, my younger image climbed back down from the top of the tree.

My image walked over and stood about twenty feet away from the little girl coming out from behind the bushes. It was Jenny's image, and the moment I saw this, everything about that day came back to me in a flurry.

"Hi," my image said, smiling.

"You climb good," the Jenna-image replied, also smiling.

My image puffed up a little. I remembered how great she'd made me feel when she'd said that. "It was nothin'."

"You did better than Johnny."

My image shrugged. "I don't get a chance to climb at my place. Not enough good trees in the neighborhood."

She nodded. "I'm Jenna."

"I'm Bill."

My image moved closer and began staring at her.

"How'd you get the black eye?"

She stopped smiling and pushed some hair across her face. "I fell."

"Really?"

"I gotta go." Then she spun around and scurried back through the woods.

My image watched her for a few moments. Then it spun around and scurried up the hill.

When I turned back to the little girl standing beside me, holding my hand, I saw that she was smiling through her tears. "Jenna, why did you bring me here?"

"You were the only one who smiled at me that day," she said. "The only one who was nice to me. Stepdad…he beat me that day…hurt my eye and gave me bruises no one else could see. He knew how and where to hit me so it wouldn't show…so the Child Protection people…so they wouldn't be suspicious. I didn't go to school for a long time because I didn't want anyone staring at my eye."

"But Jenna...if you'd gone to school, your teachers would have done something. They might have taken you away from him."

The hatred began showing behind her tears. "I didn't want to go to a state home. Besides, I didn't want anyone staring at me. They stared at me enough, made fun of me enough." She sighed. "Even your cousin did...he laughed at me, too, just like everyone else... I didn't want that. You were the only one who...the only one who ever smiled at me. The only one who was ever nice to me..."

My heart was about to shatter into little pieces. I don't know how I managed to hold myself together. I decided not to dwell on it. I needed to focus on something much more important. That had all happened in the past. Everything felt very real, but they were all shadows of events that were long gone. Past events didn't belong in the present.

This made no sense.

"Jenna, what *is* all this? Why am I here? Where did you come from? How and why did you bring us back here? This is horrible. I know it can't possibly be pleasant for you..."

She touched my hand once again.

The darkness returned.

***

When daylight returned, Jenna and I were standing at the end of the block, just a hundred yards or so from the woods separating the run-down tenement complexes from my cousin Johnny's subdivision.

It appeared to be the middle of the afternoon. At the opposite end of the block, the neighborhood playground covered most of a weed-choked, trash-littered lot. Junk cars sat in various stages of deterioration along the curb. Beer bottles, soda cans and food wrappers cluttered the sidewalk. The exhaust-laden air rang with the cries and screams of kids playing and fighting.

Once again, Jenna's hand had gone cold. She began trembling and clutched my hand tighter.

"I'm right here," I told her.

She squeezed my hand in reply.

"Jenna, why are we here?"

Silently she pointed straight ahead with her free hand.

Two figures were walking down the street, away from us. It only took me a second to realize that the figures were Johnny and myself. We were two or three years older than we'd been in the tree-climbing episode.

"This place is too noisy for me," my younger image said.

"Me, too," Johnny's younger image replied.

"Why'd you bring me here, then?"

He shrugged. "Something to do. I'm kinda bored with video games. Thought ya might like seeing the rest of the neighborhood."

"I'd rather be back in your game room, watching a movie."

Jenna turned to me. "Remember any of this?"

I tried, but nothing would come. "I remember coming here a couple of times, but nothing specific stands out."

"Just wait."

95

Three dirt-smudged punks about eleven or twelve years old walked right up to our younger images. They wore baggy pants, oversized sweatshirts, and beat-up tennies without laces. The biggest and burliest stood between them, looking us up and down. Scowling, he said, "Wanna help us beat up a kid?"

The scene suddenly began growing clearer in my memory banks as I watched it unfold.

My image turned to Johnny. "Yep. Being back at the house, sitting in your dad's recliner and watching a movie sounds really good right now."

The bully sneered at us. "Ya want to or not?"

"Five of us?" Johnny asked. "Beating up one kid?"

"Sounds kind of one-sided, doesn't it?" my image said. As I watched now, I remembered that the bully's left ear looked badly mangled. "What's wrong? You guys afraid of this kid?"

The leader moved closer and puffed out his chest. He was at least two years younger than either of us and nearly half a head shorter than me. But he still tried his best to look bigger. "Ain't afraid a nothin'!"

"Then why do you need five guys to beat up one kid?" Johnny asked flatly.

"Wanna fight?" he asked, moving closer to my image.

"Get out of my face."

His eyes blazed. "Make me!"

I'd never been a fighter, but this moron had made me angry. Besides, I didn't like anyone invading my space. He looked and smelled bad, and

I knew that if I didn't do anything, he'd force me to make a move.

Anyway, I never liked bullies—especially cowardly ones who needed help fighting their battles. I also knew that if you backed down from a bully, you'd be considered easy prey.

My arm instinctively lashed out, shoving him to the sidewalk. He landed squarely on his ass and sat there, stunned, his cronies snickering at him. Growling and rubbing his tailbone, he struggled back up, but his pants had hiked down a few inches, making it much harder to regain his footing. He took a cautious step toward me. When I refused to back away, he ran off, holding up his pants and tossing, "*Assholes*!" over his shoulder.

"You'd better run after your hero," my image said to the other two.

Without a word, they ran off in the same direction.

"Remember now?" Jenna asked, gazing up at me.

I nodded. "I guess it slipped my mind because it wasn't really that important."

"It was important to *me*," she said softly, squeezing my hand again.

"Why?"

"I was the kid they wanted to beat up. And when you ran them off…" She was smiling again.

"Why'd they want to beat you up?"

"I didn't let them push me around. Every time they pushed me, I pushed back. They even ganged up on me once and tried holding me down, all three of them, but when the leader—Viper, he called

97

himself—bent over me to spit in my face, I bit off part of his ear."

I wanted to laugh.

"I wasn't *really* mean," she said. "I just had to be tough. It wasn't a very nice neighborhood."

"I knew all about your neighborhood."

"You...don't think that was wrong, do you? Biting off his ear?"

"Not really. Besides, he had a spare ear he could always use for emergencies."

She laughed.

"Jenna?" Something had just occurred to me. "How did you know that even happened?"

She pointed to one of the junk cars parked along the curb, about twenty yards from us. The figure of a scrawny little girl knelt on the far side, just behind the front bumper. She was watching the three punks running away.

Before I could say anything else, she touched me again.

Johnny, the street, and the playground all vanished in a swirl of darkness.

CHAPTER ELEVEN

A moment later, we were standing in front of the window of Jenna's tenement apartment again.

The evening was kind of chilly, the smell of winter hovering in the air. It was late at night. Not many kids were out. Flickering lights from TVs lit up the darkness from nearly every living room window on the block.

The living room of Jenna's apartment was a horrible mess. Chairs and end-tables lay on their sides. Books, video tapes and magazines had been strewn everywhere. A wall clock lay on its back on the carpet, its face smashed. The floor was littered with beer cans, napkins, food wrappings and shattered knickknacks. A floor lamp, its dirty white shade half-crushed, lay across one of the tossed chairs. Oblivious to the horror that had swept through the room, the TV kept on playing, providing the only light source in the room.

The worst of this horror lay on the floor, near the archway leading to the hall.

Jenna's stepfather sprawled face-down on top of her small, slender form. Neither moved.

As we watched, Jenna's tiny hand gripped mine so tightly, a sharp pain jolted up my forearm. Her hand turned ice-cold; her body shivered. I looked down at her. Her face was stained with tears.

"Jenna...what *happened*?"

A sniff.

"Please...tell me."

With her left hand, she pointed to the window.

Just a few seconds later, her stepfather's bloated body moved as the other Jenna pushed him off her. Once freed of the enormous weight, she rolled away. Then, pushing herself up, she struggled to her feet. Gradually regaining her balance, she gawked at the motionless body at her feet.

She was no longer a little girl. This Jenna looked about eighteen. No longer scrawny, she'd developed into an attractive young woman, and when she pulled her hair out of her eyes, I could see that she'd become a natural beauty. Her eyes remained glued to the stationary form at her feet as she fastened her belt and buttoned her blouse. Discovering some of the buttons missing, she sighed and let her arms drop. She then contemplated the swollen body for nearly a minute before covering her face with her hands.

Stunned, I turned to Jenna. She was still shaking. "You…killed him?" I whispered.

She shook her head and continued gripping my hand.

"He's dead, isn't he?"

A nod.

I realized only then that I was asking the wrong questions. But I wasn't sure how to ask the right ones. I just didn't know how to ask a young girl if her stepfather had raped her. "Did he…force himself to—"

"He tried to…he wanted me to…he—"

"I understand." There was no reason to ask for further details.

She looked up at me and sniffed. Her tear-stained eyes searched mine. "*Do* you?"

"He was a bad man, Jenna. A monster. This world is full of monsters. Monsters need to be dead, or in prison. Yes. I totally understand."

Suddenly she broke down. I turned toward her. She pressed herself against me and sobbed hysterically.

About a minute later, when the sobbing subsided, she looked up at me. "He tried to…he almost—"

"It's all right, Jenna. It's all over now. It happened a long time ago. He'll never bother you again."

"He tried to…he grabbed my neck—"

"It's all right." I didn't want to put her through this again. "You don't have to tell me everything."

"I've never…*never* told anyone…I—"

"I understand, Jenna. I really do."

"His heart…it just…gave out…"

"That was a blessing."

A nod. "I…I had to go…to leave…to get away…"

"I would have, too."

"You don't…think I'm terrible, do you?"

I stroked her hair. "No, Jenna. I could never think that."

She smiled through her tears. Then, before I realized it, we were both enveloped in darkness.

***

In the very next moment, Jenna and I were sitting beside the image of a much younger me in the back seat of a cab as the driver followed two solid lanes of fast-moving heavy traffic out of the city.

"Leavin' town for the holidays?" the cabby asked.

"I just got a terrific job offer in Florida," my younger image said, grinning proudly.

Although this had all happened twenty years earlier, I remembered the day well. It marked a major advancement in my life at a time when I really needed one. I'd graduated from Carnegie-Mellon six months earlier and had been working part-time at an investment firm on Fifth Avenue.

The money hadn't been very good, barely enough to support me and the Penn Avenue efficiency apartment I'd been living in the last three years. To make matters worse, they'd hired me primarily as a runner. As a result, I hadn't been able to learn much at all about what I really needed to know in my new profession. I'd once calculated that I'd been spending 80% of my time out of the office, delivering personal errands and top priority parcels to other companies.

I'd taken the job to get some experience while earning enough money to live on, but once I realized just what the job involved, I got right on the stick during my first week at the company, sending in my resume to more than a dozen other companies all over the country. Eight of the firms I'd applied to hadn't bothered to respond. Five others called weeks later to inform me that the position I'd applied for had already been filled.

Then, in the midst of my discouragement, I heard from Crosley, Williams, & Associates.

They'd called just a few weeks before, asking if I could fly down to Orlando the week before

Christmas for an interview. I'd told them that I didn't think I could get the time off from my present job, but when they said the interview was merely a formality and that they'd liked what they'd seen in my resume and wanted to take me on, I told them I'd be down in a few days, after I'd given my employer my notice.

"Florida, eh?" The cabby shook his head. He was a small, skinny man in his late forties or early fifties, and barely able to see above the steering wheel. His cap was pushed down on his forehead. I could see only his bushy black brows and small, blinking chestnut eyes in his rearview. "Tough to take…"

"How's that?"

He shrugged a bony shoulder. "Besides the sandy beaches, the sunshine, the eighty-five degrees eleven months of the year and the bikinis, how d'ya think you're gonna take bein' so far away from the Shangri-La we've got here? It's thirty-seven friggin' degrees out there right now, and it's s'posed to hit damn near zero by midnight."

"Florida isn't perfect, you know."

"Howzat?"

"They get hurricanes."

He snorted. "Yeah. Uh-huh. Hurricanes. Every ten years they get a whopper. The air's cleaned out, and if ya got insurance, ya get yourself a new roof and better awnings. Up here, we don't have to worry about hurricanes. We got the cool weather to keep those bad boys away. We only get ice storms and blizzards, and when we ain't freezin' to death, we're busy workin' up a sweat—not to mention a

103

good heart attack—shovelin' snow. Thirty-seven friggin' degrees, sometimes twenty below, sometimes ten…" He shook his head. "Hurricanes. Poor baby…"

"Actually, I would've taken this job if the company was in Alaska."

"Ya don't say?"

"I really would have."

He thought that over for a little while. "Must be helluva job."

"It is, from what they already told me."

"Good pay?"

"Not right off, but once I've been there for six months, they promised me a fifteen-percent raise, along with bonus options."

"Good benefits?"

"They've got *great* benefits."

"Well, grab it, then. Terrific jobs don't come easy, ya know. Got folks up here?"

"They're divorced."

He shook his head. "Makes it bad—especially for the holidays."

"It's worse when your mom and dad are together but don't want to be."

He nodded. "There's that, I guess…"

"I'll survive."

"Yeah." He chuckled. "The beaches. The bikinis."

"And don't forget the eighty-five degrees eleven months of the year."

"How could I forget somethin' like that?"

Fighting the hectic stop-and-go traffic, the cabby pulled up to the curb at the terminal at

Pittsburgh International and parked behind a PAT bus. My image got out and went to the back, where the cabby was pulling my two gray Samsonite suitcases from the trunk. I watched as I handed him his fare, then slapped a twenty-dollar-bill on top of it.

The cabby gawked at it. "What's this?"

I shrugged. "A tip—what else?"

"Ya sure about this, buddy?"

"I'm sure."

"Listen—"

"You're a nice guy. We had a good time. It's my way of saying thanks."

He sighed. "I sure didn't expect *this* much…"

"Have a nice holiday. Buy yourself something. Buy your wife something."

The cabby shook my hand and patted me on the shoulder. "Good luck in Florida, kid. You're gonna do just fine."

"I hope so. And thanks again."

Squaring my shoulders, my image picked up the suitcases and went inside the terminal.

Jenna and I followed.

As small crowds and nervous, sweating individuals rushed in front of and through us, Jenna said, "How much of that cabby ride do you remember?"

A tall, middle-aged guy in an oversized trench coat stopped between us and placed his shiny black attaché case on the floor at his feet. He reached into his coat and fished for his ticket. As he opened it and checked it closely with blinking eyes, I stepped to my right so I could see Jenna better.

"Most of it," I told her. "It was the most important trip of my life. I'd just landed my dream job and was leaving all this behind me. My parents hadn't exactly made things pleasant for me the last five years."

Jenna nodded.

"I just don't see why we're here." On my left and about twenty feet away, my image continued walking through the terminal, toward the signs that said *TICKETS*. "Don't I get my luggage checked, then walk over to the seats and wait for my flight?"

Jenna smiled. "Something else happened that day. Something important."

I could tell by her impish smile that she was holding something back. "What is it?" I asked.

Without a word, she pointed behind me.

I turned.

A tall, slender blond woman wearing sunglasses and a red scarf rushed down the hall, keeping away from the passing crowds and people staring in confusion at the signs and flight schedules. She stopped briefly in front of the large digital sign showing the flight schedules and opened her bag to check her ticket.

"Why are we watching her?" I asked.

"Just wait." Jenna's eyes stayed fixed on the woman.

A moment later, the blonde slipped the ticket back in her bag, turned and approached the gate, where signs announcing the details of the connecting flight to Los Angeles were posted on metal stands as well as overhead. She hurried through the doorway and scanned the crowd, then walked over to a vacant seat facing the windows that looked out onto the runway.

As more people slipped through us, we kept watching the solitary blonde. She sat in the curved plastic seat, her bag on the floor next to her right foot. She seemed all alone in her own little world, totally oblivious of what was going on around her while staring at the planes taking off and landing on the other side of the huge window.

While we watched, a skinny young guy around nineteen in a wrinkled black windbreaker, jeans and athletic shoes emerged from the crowd, shuffled over to the window, and stood about three feet from her. He seemed to be watching the activity outside as well. Just as the blonde reached up to adjust the scarf covering her hair, the boy snatched her bag, spun around and bolted toward the hall. Catching the activity only a second later, the blonde jumped up and ran after him.

I couldn't believe what I'd just seen. "What the hell's going on?"

"Look behind you."

I turned around. My other image was standing about fifty feet away, just a few feet from the sign announcing the flights. The strap of the blonde's leather bag was gripped in my left hand. The kid lay squirming on the floor at my feet, clutching his stomach.

"Does any of this ring a bell?" Jenna asked.

"I vaguely remember." I recalled the incident, but I still couldn't shake the confusion. "What does any of this have to do with—"

"*Sshhh*!"

107

Witnessing the sight, the blonde stopped cold in her tracks. Then, realizing what just happened, she rushed over. When she was about five feet away from me, she stopped and watched the security guards scrambling to grab the punk and drag him away.

After a few tense moments, she recovered. Shaking herself, she gazed at my younger self as if in a trance.

I held out her bag. "I believe this is yours."

She didn't reply; she just stared at me.

"You okay? That jerk didn't hurt you, did he?"

Still staring, she shook her head. Then she slowly reached out and cautiously took her bag.

My younger image showed obvious concern. "Are you in shock or something? I can probably find a doctor, but in this crowd, it might take a while, and by the time someone gets his butt over here, you'll probably miss your flight…"

"No…" She shook her head again. "I'm all right. I'm just fine…thanks to you."

After a moment, my image said, "Do I…know you?"

The blonde didn't reply. After a long pause, she said, "How can I ever thank you…for this…for what you've done?"

"It's not necessary. I just happened to see what he did and had to stop him. A hard fist to the gut usually works wonders."

She continued staring.

My image stared back. Now that this was all unfolding before me again, I recalled that I was trying to evaluate the situation. I also recalled that

108

this girl looked familiar, and it irritated me that I couldn't remember how I knew her. "Are you *sure* we don't know one another?"

"I'm sure. And thank you. I'll never forget this…as long as I live."

"It's all right. I just happened to be there when he—"

"You've been so…so *good* to me. I can *never* thank you enough…"

My image didn't reply. I could clearly see the total confusion on my face. Finally, my younger self said, "It wasn't anything, really. I just tripped him as he ran past, and when he tried getting back up, I—"

"Thank you *so* much…for everything…"

"You're very welcome. And best of luck to you."

She gazed at me a few more seconds, then turned and slowly walked back to the waiting area.

My image continued watching her, scratching the back of my neck as she disappeared in the crowd down the hall.

"You're confused," Jenna said.

"Extremely."

"Was it because she was staring at you?"

"It was because she looked so familiar. And, of course, because she was so *grateful*…"

"You were there for her."

"As I told her, I just—"

"It was much more than that."

"All I did was stop some asshole from stealing her bag. Anyone else would've done the same thing."

"Why do you think she looked so familiar?"

I didn't reply. I still had no idea what was going on. Jenna obviously knew. Otherwise, she wouldn't have brought me here. "Please tell me what that was all about, Jenna."

"You still haven't figured it out yet?"

"I guess I'm just a little dense about some things."

"Do you really want to know why she seemed so familiar?"

"More than you could ever possibly know."

"Take a look at her again."

I turned back to the doorway. The crowd gathering at the window in front of the line of plastic chairs concealed the blonde from me. "I can't see her now—"

"This was why," came her reply in a different voice.

Startled, I turned.

Little Jenna had suddenly transformed into a beautiful young woman with a shapely figure, long blond hair and a captivating smile.

"J-Jenna?" I couldn't believe my eyes.

"It's me."

I tossed a thumb to my right, where the blonde had disappeared. "That was...that was *you*?"

A nod.

Once again I found myself at a total loss. Even though I now knew what happened, I still found that I couldn't quite grasp what was actually going on. "Why didn't you *tell* me who you were? Why didn't you—"

"I tried to. I really did. I wanted you to know how much you…what you did…what you really meant to me…"

"But you didn't. I would've loved knowing what happened. I would've loved knowing who you were. Why didn't you give me at least a *clue*?"

"It's a long story."

I shrugged. "I'm here, and so are you. Don't forget, you brought me here. And I'm listening."

Still smiling, she stared at me.

The darkness came back once again.

CHAPTER TWELVE

Once the darkness had burned away, we were walking down a deserted street that went up a hill.

It seemed late in the morning. Jenna kept close beside me. As beautiful as she was, I missed the sweet little girl who'd showed me so much of her troubled past and I found that I couldn't stop hoping she'd change back.

As we walked, I kept looking for familiar signs of where we were. The neighborhood seemed oddly familiar. The steep hills and slopes leading down to the valley behind the two- and three-story brick homes on the right side of the paved road told me we were still in the Pittsburgh area. But even though I had some idea of where this was, our reason for being here remained a mystery.

I strongly suspected that the main issue had nothing to do with our actual whereabouts, and that the reason for all this awaited us at the top of the hill, just beyond this development.

"I'm still right here with you," I told her as we walked. "And I'm still curious about why you took me to the airport."

"That happened two years after...my stepdad...after I—"

"What happened with that? Did you get in trouble?"

"As I told you before, it wasn't murder." As she spoke, she continued staring straight ahead at the hill veering off to our left. "He'd been drinking all day, and when I came home from school, he was

112

waiting for me. He was worse than…than I'd ever seen him before." She stopped walking; her eyes glistened in the sunlight. "He'd touched me before. Many times."

"I saw him hit you. Is that what you mean?"

She turned and gazed at me. I could see the anger, the hatred, and the hurt in her eyes. I could only imagine how much damage that bastard had done to her. "He…did both. When I came home that day, it was different. I saw something in his eyes I'd never seen before. I actually thought I saw death in them. My death. I felt very cold. The darkness on his face and the strange smell coming from him that day scared me worse than anything I'd ever been through. It was like…like he'd turned into a wild beast." She resumed walking.

"Did his mind just snap?" I asked, catching up to her.

"I don't know what happened. I only know that whatever was coming out of him that day wasn't anything I'd ever known before."

I didn't reply.

"He'd worked himself up to rape me, and when I came home, he was blind drunk and all over me. And before I knew what was happening, he'd pushed me down to the floor, straddled me and ripped my blouse open. I struggled with him as much as I could, but he was big and heavy and, as I just said, wild. I got my hands on his throat and tried hard to strangle him, but it was too much for me. His neck…it was so *thick*…so *solid*. I could hardly get my fingers in there and do what I…" She sighed and went silent.

113

After nearly a minute of silence, I said, "We've come this far… Tell me what happened next."

She shrugged. "He just stopped moving. His face was mashed against the top of my head, and just when I thought I was gonna suffocate and die, he moaned and kinda snorted—almost like a snore—and the next thing I knew, he got really heavy."

"You said it was his heart?"

"It was weak from all the booze, and he just collapsed on me and died. I lay there the longest time, thinking he'd just passed out. But after a while, I could tell something was different. I could no longer feel his heart thumping against me, and the hot breath coming out of his nostrils had stopped. When I finally got the courage to take my hands away from his neck, I searched for a pulse."

"He died before you had the chance to kill him."

"I wanted to. I really did. I wanted to *so* badly…"

"I can't say as I blame you."

"Once they came and took him away, I knew I couldn't stay there, so I got in touch with my brother Danny and asked if I could stay with him and his wife Sharon. I stayed with them for about six months or so, but that didn't turn out very well. Sharon didn't really want me with them and made it clear that I was cramping their lifestyle. I'd been waiting tables all this time, saving up as much money as I could. Since I'd spent so much time staying away from home in those days, I didn't have much of an education, so I took my GED and tried

114

to get a better job. I thought I had one, but the guy who'd hired me hadn't hired me for the right reasons, and I had to leave that place right away."

"What were you doing at the airport?"

"I needed to get away from this area. I thought maybe I'd have better luck if I was living somewhere else. I decided to try my hand at working at the movie studios in Hollywood. Not acting, of course—doing makeup and stuff like that. I'd always been good at makeup and even set designing. After all, I'd been covering up my bruises since I was little. Applying makeup was really no big deal for me. And I'd always had an eye for arranging furniture and making things look really good.

"I'd helped design a set at our high school for one of their plays. Everyone liked what I'd done and said it really looked professional. It was my first attempt, so I figured maybe I had the knack for it. I decided to take a gamble and head off to L.A. and try my luck out there. As I said, I'd saved up a lot of money, enough for a one-way plane ticket and a month's rent. That's what I did. I took every cent that I'd saved and used it for my trip. Then I got on the plane and flew to L.A."

I didn't want to ask but knew I had to. "How did it turn out?"

She smiled. "It was all right for a while, but after eight months or so, it fizzled out. I just didn't have the drive, I guess. I'd never been very aggressive with people—which is how you have to be when you're out there. You also have to be very self-confident—which was something else I never

115

had. I landed a few jobs and even managed to get on a couple of movie sets, making up some of the extras. I made a little money for a while. I met a lot of guys, too. A lot of bad ones." She went silent again, withdrawing quickly into her own little world.

"Tell me the rest, Jenna."

"One of them turned out to be a real bastard— even worse than my stepdad. He was about thirty, good-looking, and ran a car dealership." She paused, and when she spoke again, her voice sounded much weaker. "He liked rough sex and especially loved batting women around. He beat me up during one of our dates. First, he slapped me around. Then he punched me in the kidney—the same place my stepdad had punched me just a few years earlier. My kidneys were both already damaged from all the beatings and from the leather belt my stepdad had whacked me with, so..." She sighed. "I just couldn't take much more."

A flurry of seething anger rushed through me like a ruptured water main. I had to clear my throat to get the words out. "How bad...were you hurt?"

"*Real* bad." She took a breath and looked down at her feet. "I suffered uremic poisoning a few days later and died of cerebral edema one week after that."

The tears filled my eyes. I turned away. I couldn't look at her; I needed some time to absorb all this and collect myself. But just a moment later, her hand gripped mine again. I turned back to her. Her eyes were also wet, but she was smiling. "Are you okay?" she asked.

"I'm *so* sorry, Jenna…" I had no other words to express.

She smiled. "Do you really want to know why I took you to the airport?"

"Please…tell me."

"I'd made a promise to myself that morning. I promised myself that this trip to L.A. would be a one-time thing. Nothing in my life had ever gone right up until then, and if one more bad thing happened before I got on that plane, I'd just turn right around and take a cab back home."

I suddenly realized that it had been because of me that she'd died in L.A. "So…your trip to L.A…if I hadn't given you back your bag…"

"The moment I saw that jerk running away with it, I knew that I'd made a big mistake—that I wasn't supposed to go anywhere. In that one instant, I knew that I was going back home. I told myself I'd never amount to nothing, and there was no need for me to try anything else ever again."

She went silent for a few moments. "But I had to at least try and get my bag back first. It had all my valuables in it. I had no idea how I could possibly get it back from that jerk, but I had to try. I told myself that if I didn't at least try, it would be a definite sign that I didn't have what it takes to do anything. I didn't want to spend the rest of my life hating myself for not going after him or wondering what might have been if I *had* gone after him. So I jumped up and was about to rush through the doorway when I saw you standing there, holding my bag, with him lying at your feet." She smiled. "For me, it was a sign straight from Heaven that I should

117

go on." Her eyes searched his. "Don't you see the significance of all this? The fact that you were there the same moment I was? That even though so much time had gone by, we still managed to connect one last time?"

"But Jenna…your future…the fact that you died not long after that…" I couldn't help feeling guilty for what happened to her once she'd gotten on the plane and flown to L.A.

She was still smiling. "You did more for me that day than anyone else had ever done. You showed me more kindness those few times I saw you than I'd ever experienced before, and if you hadn't stopped that guy, I would have gone back home and ended up living in someone's basement, turning tricks."

"Instead, you went to L.A…and died—"

"I died after I'd done what I promised myself I was going to do. Yes, I died much too soon, and no, I didn't get to do most of what I wanted to…but if I hadn't gotten on that plane…" She shrugged.

"Jenna, if you'd just told me who you were that day—"

"What would you have done? Changed your plans? Turned your back on your future? Turned down that dream job you'd worked all those years for? Gone all out to do something else for me? You'd already done enough. You gave me hope. You showed me that there was kindness in the world—that not all men were savages and predators. You gave me the courage to venture out on my own and pursue my dream. If it hadn't been for you, I wouldn't have even taken my GED in the first place. You might not know it, but if you hadn't looked at me the way you did or stood up for me those few times we ran into one another, I would have never known that I even deserved any self-respect."

I could feel what was left of my reserve beginning to crumble.

"Do you know what my last thoughts were, just before I died?"

I was afraid to ask.

"I promised myself that if I could, I was going to find some way to repay you for what you'd done for me."

I had no idea how to respond.

Still gripping my hand, she led me up the hill, where Mount Lebanon Cemetery stood at the very top. We went up a narrow dirt road, turned left, slipped past a small grove of trees and approached a polished gray marble marker set in the overgrown grass, just ten feet or so from a large oak tree.

The marker said, simply:

JENNA RAE CAULFIELD
1976-1999

As I gazed at it, my eyes filled with more tears.

"When my brothers were notified about what happened, they made arrangements to have me brought back here. "

"Really?" I was surprised they'd made such a kind gesture. But I knew it was much too late.

"I was surprised, too," she said with a half-smile. "I think they felt guilty for what happened."

"But not for leaving you there with your stepdad?"

She shrugged. "They were all older than I was. Rick was seventeen, so he was all set to leave home when Mom died. Danny was sixteen, Mike fifteen. They'd wanted to take me with them, but…" She shook her head. "It was just too much. They all had their own problems. I really couldn't blame them. And by the time I was able to leave and stay with Danny, he'd already begun his new life with Sharon, and they didn't need me around to complicate things. My other two brothers also had busy lives of their own."

I didn't want to say what I was feeling. Accusations were no good now. It was much too late for justice or ill will. "Well, at least they brought you back…"

She nodded. "It meant a lot. Mom's buried right there, next to my sister Pauline." She pointed to the markers lying in the grass just a few feet away.

Once again, I kept my feelings to myself.

"I've been watching over you ever since," she said, smiling at me.

I was surprised. "You haven't crossed over yet?"

She shook her head. "I made a promise. I can't cross over until I fulfill it."

"Jenna, what have you been doing—"

"As I said, I've been with you."

The realization shocked me. "You've been with me since…since the day you died?"

"I was with you in Florida and when you flew back here. I was also with you when you were mugged and dragged into that alley behind Gino's. I've been watching you while trying to stay out of the picture, but when you were dragged into the alley and it looked like something really bad was about to happen, I had to step in. I couldn't possibly let anything happen to you."

Then it dawned on me. She'd been the voice all along.

"*You* were the voice that helped me…"

"Guilty as charged."

"You also must have been the one making the nine-one-one call—"

"I had to get you to the hospital, didn't I?"

Confusion set in again. "How could you possibly make a phone call if…if you're—"

"We can do a great many things when we have to—especially in an emergency." She shrugged. "We can also make sudden sounds when we need certain mortals to look the other way at the right time. I had to distract those thugs so I could get you out of there."

"And you also knew about E&S, obviously…"

"As I said, I've been with you a long time."

"I should've known." I felt stupid for not figuring this out sooner.

She smiled. "You had no idea what was happening. You hadn't seen me since we were kids. You can't count that episode at the airport because you had no idea that was me. The bleached hair made things even more complicated."

"Why *did* you bleach your hair?"

121

She shrugged. "A new look, silly. I wanted to start a new life. But you're missing the point. In the alley, you couldn't have possibly known it was me talking to you because you didn't even know I was dead in the first place. Even if you did know, you couldn't have known that I'd been watching over you ever since I died."

Once again, the realization slammed into me. "You've actually been watching over me...all this time?"

She nodded.

"For seventeen years?"

"Time is much different on the other side. For us, a year goes by in an instant, a decade in a single afternoon. When we're busy doing something in the mortal world, the moment go by slowly. Time is but a ripple, separating special moments. But it was a real pleasure because I didn't mind being with you—not at all." She smiled. "It was the least I could do."

I was experiencing a genuine warmth for this gentle soul, one I'd never felt for anyone else before in my life. "You saved my life. I'm sure you know that."

Another nod.

"I'll never forget you, Jenna. I'll never forget any of this."

"I know that, too."

I knew right then that our time together was rapidly drawing to a close. I struggled hard to keep the sadness from taking over. "Then I guess you can cross over now. I think I'll be all right from now on."

122

She shook her head. "Not quite yet. There's something else I have to do."

"What's that?"

"Before I can cross over, I have to release you."

"*Release* me?"

"Haven't you ever wondered why you've never married? Why you've always shied away from any permanent commitment?"

I shrugged. "I'm not an easy guy—"

"Don't give me that. You can't possibly lie to *me*, Bill. You're the best man I ever knew. You'd be an absolute dream to live with."

"Jenna, you really don't—"

"You never married because of me."

"I…don't understand."

"I told you that I've been watching over you all these years, but I didn't tell you the times I've actually interfered with your life during all this time."

"Interfered?"

She lowered her head. "There were several women you could have easily taken to the altar, but because of me, it never happened."

"How can that be?"

She shrugged a shoulder. "I didn't like any of them."

I didn't understand what she was saying. "So? I didn't like them, either."

"Yes you did. That's why you were engaged to them. But none of these engagements worked out, did they?"

"A couple of them changed their minds. Then I changed *my* mind—"

"Why, Bill? Why *did* you change your mind?"

"I don't know…" Just a few months ago, Sarah had been a strong choice, but a week or so into our engagement, I decided that I couldn't imagine sharing the rest of my life with her. "I was engaged to a lady named Sarah. She—"

"The tall, slender redhead? The one who did paralegal work in Orlando?"

"How did you—"

"I was right there with you. I saw everything you did."

I gawked at her. "Everything?"

She laughed. "Don't be embarrassed. She was actually a very good choice. Your best choice, in fact."

"Then what happened? Why'd I change my mind?"

"That was my fault. I was watching you as you slept one night, and something came over me. I'm sorry, Bill. I couldn't help it, but I bent over you and kissed you. It was all very innocent, of course— just a peck on the cheek—but as I said, I just couldn't help myself."

I was stunned and extremely uncomfortable.

Jenna gazed at me the longest time before she started talking again. "I'm afraid my kiss did something that I wasn't expecting. It caused your subconscious to come to me as you slept."

My cheeks reddened, and suddenly I knew exactly what she was talking about.

"You remember, don't you? I can see it in your eyes. You've had dreams with faceless women you couldn't identify, haven't you?"

"Many times..."

"Didn't you ever wonder who I was?"

"It was you all along?"

Jenna smiled in embarrassment. "I just couldn't help myself."

It cleared up a lot of things, but it still didn't tell me how Jenna had been responsible for all my engagements breaking up. "All right, you came to me in my dreams. And by the way, they were really terrific dreams. But how did that change my relationships?"

"The subconscious is a strange thing. I was spending time with you the only way I could. Maybe your subconscious caught it and convinced you that you weren't one hundred percent ready to marry anyone else."

This made me wonder about all the other sudden decisions I'd made in the past. "Jenna...how many times did you actually share my dreams with me?"

"Too many to count. My self-control wasn't very strong in those days, and I was still very much indebted to you...and, of course, quite taken. I've liked you ever since I first saw you climb that oak tree. I'm sure you knew that then."

"I think I might have been too young to think about things like that at the time. Back then, I liked climbing trees, watching movies and playing video games. I didn't really think too much about girls until I was a little older."

"Things were much different with me. I'd been forced to grow up much faster than most other kids, so my hormones were already all set up and working by the time I first saw you. And when I saw you years later, at the airport…well, that turned out to be the icing on the cake. I knew I was in love with you then. I also knew it was impossible to do anything about it."

"So now you're releasing me?"

A nod. "We're square, now, and I can cross over without any feelings of guilt, or remorse."

I felt a lump gathering in my throat. "And I'll never see you again…"

She blinked, and another tear drifted down her cheek. "Not in *this* life…"

A sudden strong sense of sadness made me empty inside.

She reached out and took my hand one last time. "Would you do one last favor for me?"

"Anything."

"One last kiss?"

I could feel more tears gathering. "I'm guessing you don't want it on the cheek this time…"

Without warning, she came closer and planted a tender kiss on my lips. I put my arms around her, but she'd already begun fading.

"Bye, Bill." Her face was very close to mine. "Thank you for saving me…and for being there when I needed you."

"And thank you for saving me, Jenna."

Although she was nearly invisible, she still managed to squeeze my hand one last time. "Now you can meet some lucky woman and spend the rest of your life with her."

I couldn't bear watching her disappear so quickly. "Jenna, please don't—"

"I like Brittany. She's very nice. I think the two of you were actually meant for one another."

"Jenna, what can I do to—"

"Get married, Bill. Be happy. That's the best thing I can wish for you right now. And don't worry. I'll never interfere again. I promise that the next time we meet, it won't be in a dream."

The pressure on my hand disappeared.

Before she vanished, I caught one last wave, and the darkness returned.

I opened my eyes.

I was sitting on the park bench, my cup of steaming hot cocoa warming my hands. Brittany was walking back from the Christmas tree, her beautiful green eyes fixed on me with every step she took.

CHAPTER THIRTEEN

"I was afraid you'd abandoned me."

Brittany looked worried and confused as she sat down beside me.

I looked around to get my bearings.

The same crowd. The same carolers. Apparently nothing had changed since Jenna had pulled me into the past with her. It seemed like I'd been gone for several hours, but something told me I wasn't gone very long at all.

"Really?" Instinct told me to act surprised. I guessed that if I told her what had really happened, she'd run for cover. "You actually thought I *left* you?"

She had a sip of hot cocoa and shivered a little from the cold. "I was checking out one of the ornaments. It was really cute. A Norman Rockwell Santa—right out of one of his paintings. I wanted you to see it, but when I turned to yell for you to join me, you weren't here."

"Are you saying I was gone?"

"Of course not. Throngs of people were walking by, and when I glanced over here, I thought I saw an empty bench. But when a group of older people passed just a few seconds later, there you were. I guess it was just my imagination."

I feigned anger. "You actually thought I'd leave you here? All alone? With these strangers wandering around?"

She reddened. "That was kind of paranoid, wasn't it?"

"Slightly, but I'll forgive you—this time."

She patted my forearm. "I'm truly sorry. You were out of my sight for what was probably no more than just a few seconds and I was all set to panic."

"Do you usually panic on all your dates?"

She smiled. "Only when I think I've been abandoned…"

"Has that ever happened?"

"Not yet…"

"Good. There *is* hope for the male species, after all."

She laughed and brushed up against me.

A few seconds. I was only gone a few seconds. I'd been pulled from the land of the living by Jenna's spirit, taken back to our childhood, then to Mount Lebanon Cemetery, where her body had been laid to rest nearly two decades ago…

All this in just seconds.

It seemed so unreal.

The whole thing was incredible. In fact, this entire trip had turned dreamlike from the moment I was mugged…up until that very special kiss I'd shared with the ghost of a beautiful woman I would have fallen in love with, married, and shared the rest of my life with, had the circumstances been different.

However, it was never to be.

But in spite of knowing what happened and what didn't happen, I knew that I'd never forget Jenna, nor would I ever forget what she'd given me.

Just a few seconds of my life had changed my destiny forever.

A lifetime had been shared…in just moments.

"Time is much different on the other side."

It certainly was. In just a few seconds of mortal time, she'd shown me love…and admiration…and respect…and the longing of one heart for another… But most of all, a burning desire for gratitude that had survived the tragically short lifetime of a gentle soul, even after death…

"Time is but a ripple, separating special moments…"

It was so difficult to imagine.

"You're awfully quiet," Brittany said. "Is something wrong?"

"I think the two of you were actually meant for one another."

"No." I placed my hand on hers. "As a matter of fact, for the first time in my life, everything is totally right."

Brittany moved closer to me and gazed into my eyes. Her voice was soft, but the message was clear. "What would you like to do now, Bill?"

I smiled. "Something I've wanted to do ever since I first laid eyes on you."

"Really?" Her eyes grew. "What's that?"

"A gentleman never reveals his private thoughts…"

She kissed me, and when she pulled away, she kept her face very close. "Forget the gentleman thing, okay? Just tell me what you wanna do."

"I'd like to spend Christmas Eve with you."

She blinked. "But…you already are."

130

I looked into her eyes and lowered my voice to a whisper. "Yes, but I'd like to keep doing it until it becomes Christmas."

We kissed again.

Many moments later, she stood and took my hand.

Then we hurried out of the Square and went back to where she'd parked her Lexus.

CHAPTER FOURTEEN

The next morning, after Brittany and I enjoyed a wonderful breakfast of scrambled eggs with melted cheese and diced ham, rye toast, croissants, and cinnamon-flavored coffee, I asked her to help me find a florist that would be open on Christmas Day.

She asked no questions. This, of course, convinced me that she really was a terrific, understanding lady. After nearly an hour of checking the local floral shops in the Yellow Pages, we found a small place on McKnight Road that was open until noon. I bought a bouquet of a dozen fresh white roses and gave a twenty-dollar tip to the daughter of the owner, the sweet girl who'd help me pick it out and took special care wrapping it up.

Twenty minutes later, Brittany and I were off to Mt. Lebanon.

At ten o'clock, traffic was nearly non-existent. On Christmas morning, everyone is too busy exchanging and opening gifts, having breakfast, or sleeping in, to spend time on the highway.

It took just half an hour to reach the cemetery and only a few minutes to find Jenna's marker. I was soon standing over her stone once again, my head spinning with images of what happened the previous evening. As before, I found myself weakening when the realization hit me. Jenna had actually returned from the dead not only to save my life, but also to show me what had happened to her and how much I'd truly meant to her.

132

The instant I felt my self-control crumbling, I forced myself to hold it all together. Jenna wouldn't want me to crumble—not now, and especially not in front of Brittany. So I collected myself. I stared at her name on the marker while inwardly hoping against hope that time would do its thing yet again to create that special ripple that would bring Jenna back once more. I knew this was foolish, but it was how I felt.

I closed my eyes and visualized her face. At first, she appeared as little Jenna. Then, in the next instant, she'd changed once again into grown-up Jenna, and she was smiling at me. And as she smiled, I was convinced I could hear her voice. She was telling me to be happy...to get married...and that she would never forget me.

Just then, a warm hand gripped mine, and I cringed and turned sharply.

Brittany stood beside me, smiling. Once the tense moment had passed, I managed to return her smile. I hoped she wouldn't be able to tell by my tense expression that she'd nearly given me a heart attack—that for one brief instant, I'd thought Jenna had actually come back.

Brittany's beaming smile showed only warmth and contentment.

Whether I liked it or not, I was back in the present. However, things weren't as bleak as they could have been. A beautiful woman was standing beside me. She'd brought me here so I could bring flowers to a dead young woman I'd never really known...a young woman who, unbeknownst to me, had been watching over me nearly half my life.

As I looked down upon Jenna's grave, I felt the tears coming again but forced myself to concentrate on the issue at hand. My thoughts were simple, but heartfelt: "*Jenna, I know I just saw you last night, but I just had to come back and pay my respects. I know I'll never be able to properly thank you for what you've done for me or even begin to understand everything that happened between us. But I know what I saw and what I felt, and all I can say is that when my time comes, I hope with all my heart that I'll see you again.*"

Sighing from the effort, I knelt on the cold, snow-dusted ground and placed the bouquet of roses on her stone. Once I felt more tears gathering, I wiped them away and straightened.

"May I ask?" Brittany whispered, coming closer.

I knew then that it was time to let Brittany know what was going on, so I nodded.

"Girlfriend from your past?"

From my past, present, and future, I wanted to say. But I knew better than say something like that to a woman I'd just met only days ago and already cared very much for. "If I'd paid more attention to her, I would have probably fallen in love with her."

Brittany stared at me the longest time before she responded. "Would it be terrible of me to say that I'm really glad things turned out the way they did?"

I smiled at her. "I'm really glad things turned out this way, too."

Brittany went silent. Then she placed her hand in mine and turned to gaze at Jenna's marker. "She must have been a special lady."

"She was. Very special."

"How did she die? Or shouldn't I ask?"

"It's a long story."

Her beautiful green eyes stayed on me. "I hope you'll tell me all about her one day."

In that one moment I saw something in those eyes I'd only seen once before. I'd seen it in Jenna's eyes just before she'd kissed me, and I knew right then that Jenna had been right. Brittany and I were meant to be together.

"I will," I told her, and she smiled and squeezed my hand.

"Jenna *must* have been truly special," she said. "You've never forgotten her."

"Actually, she's always been with me."

"Should I be jealous?"

"She wouldn't want you to be."

"How can you be so sure?"

"Because she likes you."

"What?"

Realizing what I'd just said, I sighed. "I meant...she *would've* liked you."

Brittany gave my hand a slight tug. "Let's go back to my place. It's Christmas Day. She wouldn't want you to spend Christmas Day here, would she?"

"She'd want me to enjoy myself."

"Let's go, then."

I stared at the rose-covered marker one last time. "*I'll never forget you, Jenna. You'll always be in my heart.*"

Brittany nudged me once again, and we turned and went back down the hill, where her silver Lexus awaited us.

Just as I climbed in, I could have sworn I heard Jenna's voice in my head. It sounded like she was saying, "*Be happy, Bill, and I'll see you again, one day.*"

Fresh tears gathered in my eyes as Brittany started up the car and eased away from the curb.

THE END

OTHER WORKS BY DAVID BERARDELLI

THE APPRENTICE
THE WAGON DRIVER
DEMONCHASER I
DEMONCHASER II
STEPPING OUT OF MY GRAVE
ESCAPE CLAUSE
FATAL INNOCENCE
THE FUNNY DETECTIVE
JUST A SIMPLE ERRAND
COLORS
WORKING FOR A MOB BOSS
AND DARKNESS FELL
AFTER DARKNESS FELL
DEMONCHASER III
ENLIGHTENMENT
IN ANOTHER REALM
BEYOND RECOGNITION
LOOKING FOR A DEAD GUY
THE NIGHTMARE COLLECTOR
HIDDEN
YESTERDAY'S JOURNEY
BEYOND GUILT
AWAKENED

Titles available through:
Fiction4All